A WORKOUT THAT WILL WORK OUT

Sally Jones is an Iron Man athlete. She holds a BTec in sports and exercise science from Stockport College, UK, and was captain of the Tameside netball team, Manchester, UK. She is a level-3 personal trainer from Active IQ, UK and co-founder of Multifit Wellness, one of the fastest growing functional fitness brands in the world. In 2019, she received the Business World Young Entrepreneur of the Year award.

Samir Kapoor has a PhD in management from Symbiosis International University. He is also a level-3 personal trainer from Active IQ, UK and co-founder of Multifit Wellness. Being an army kid, he was always interested in adventure sports. Samir loves to trek, and has trekked to the Mt Everest base camp a couple of times.

Advance Praise for *A Workout that Will Work Out*

'This book is a great way to help those already involved in fitness gain a greater understanding about what they are doing and why they are doing it. It clearly outlines information with precise instructions and great illustrations.'

– Luke Lenon Ford, sprinter, European Athletics U23 Championships gold and bronze medallist

'So many athletes do exercises that don't improve their own performance. This book helps you find the exercises that suit your needs so you can gain from your workout.'

– Chris Tomlinson, long jumper, Olympian, European Athletics Championships bronze and World Indoor Championships silver medallist

'This is a simple yet very effective book for those who are already into some kind of training regimen and, most importantly, for those who are uninitiated and looking for ways and means to get clarity on "what fitness is all about and what all they can get out of it". Easy to understand with more than adequate illustrations and pictures to aid the reader.'

– Andy Turner, hurdler, Olympian, World Championships bronze, Commonwealth Games gold and bronze, European Championships gold and bronze and European Team Championships gold medallist

'I think there is a need for such an easy-to-understand breakdown of the fitness journey for those who are already on it or indeed have just begun! I love that the book breaks down concisely what functional fitness is and just how relevant it is for everyone because it encapsulates movements we use every single day! Laying the right foundation and habits is key. This book challenges a fitness beginner's mindset and helps them understand getting "fit for purpose and fit for life".'

– Marilyn Okoro, track and field athlete, Olympian, Olympic bronze, IAAF World Championships bronze, European Athletics Championships silver medallist

'Definitely a seminal work by Samir and Sally, who have put all their experience of training thousands of people across the world and their definitive knowledge of the craft of fitness into this compact compendium of fitness. Brilliant indeed.'

– Manoj Pingale, boxer, Olympian, Arjuna awardee

A WORKOUT THAT WILL WORK OUT

SAMIR KAPOOR
SALLY JONES

HarperCollins *Publishers* India

First published in India in 2019 by
HarperCollins *Publishers*
A-75, Sector 57, Noida, Uttar Pradesh 201301, India
www.harpercollins.co.in

2 4 6 8 10 9 7 5 3 1

P-ISBN: 978-93-5357-090-3
E-ISBN: 978-93-5357-091-0

Typeset in 11.5/15.2 Sabon LT Std at
Manipal Digital Systems, Manipal

Printed and bound at
Thomson Press (India) Ltd

MIX
Paper
FSC FSC® C010615

This book is produced from independently certified FSC® paper to ensure responsible forest management.

Contents

Foreword vii

Preface ix

1. Military Training and Its Components 1
2. Self-evaluation and Formulating a Personal Fitness Plan 10
3. Functional Fitness Defined 20
4. Fitness Fundas: Components of Body Fitness 34
5. Basic Blocks of Functional Training 56
6. Criterion for Effective Training 242
7. Rifle Workout 253

Nutrition 256

Glossary of Fitness Terms 280

Foreword

I LOVED SPORTS as a child and still love them, and was fortunate to receive the honour of playing cricket for my country. Within a month of retirement from cricket in 1994, I started playing golf.

I was very happy to see Samir and Sally, both qualified fitness professionals, who have trained thousands of people come up with a simple and yet very effective book, aptly titled *A Workout that Will Work Out*. With their knowledge and years of experience running a chain of functional fitness gyms across three continents, they are the perfect people to teach us about functional fitness. The best thing about this book is that it can be easily understood and implemented by even an uninitiated person. And it gives basic information on nutrition as well.

I strongly recommend that you pick up this book, read it, absorb it and then hit a gym!

I wish Samir and Sally good luck and congratulate them for bringing out such a wonderful book.

New Delhi
1 May 2019

Kapil Dev

Preface

'A workout that will work out.'—TM

THERE ARE THOUSANDS of books already out there that help fitness enthusiasts achieve the body shape and fitness level they want. So why write another one? In our observation, we realized that most of these books assume that the person picking them up has an established fitness regimen and is familiar with the basics of working out. But what about those looking to step into the world of physical fitness and workout regimes for the first time?

We wanted to bring out a simple yet effective book for those who are just starting out in this sphere and are looking for ways and means to get clarity on what fitness is and what they can get out of a good workout. This uninitiated group is the most important audience, because they need to be educated on the basics of a good workout regime right from the beginning, so that they do not randomly pick up exercises that turn out to be unsuitable (i.e., that might damage their bodies instead of making them more fit), and then attempt a course correction when it is too late. With exercise, like golfing or swimming, if you pick up a wrong style, you will end up getting frustrated after a while because it will not yield the results you want in the long run. (In fact, a wrong exercise can end up damaging your muscles instead of strengthening them!) And then when you realize that you've been doing it wrong all this time and go for a change of style, it will most likely take four times the effort it would have if you had *started* right—because now you need to unlearn, and relearn from scratch.

When the fitness industry was in its nascent years, machines took the spotlight. It was believed that the more the machines in a gym, the better the facility that gym provided. Treadmills, steppers and the like were seen in every gym. All you had to do was use those machines and you would be fitter in no time!

In contrast, the training out on the field for the armed forces saw barely any change in its methods.

Yet gym equipment has its share of pros and cons. Take, for example, the treadmill, the most popular workout equipment across the world, a staple for all gyms.

In 2014, *Time* magazine came out with an article on the pros and cons of treadmills. As per the article, running on the treadmill is easier on your joints than running on hard pavement, you can control the difficulty level and include the effects of air resistance by increasing the incline; and more advanced machines even allow you to simulate a custom race environment.

But on the downside, treadmills fail to mimic real-life conditions of running on uneven ground. This redundancy can lead to slip-ups due to negligence, increasing the chances of injury, or induce such boredom that one loses the motivation to exercise. One also doesn't use as many muscles on a treadmill as are required in running outdoors on uneven ground, in rounding corners, etc.

So we come to the question at hand: What is the best fitness regimen to follow in order to remain healthy and fit for life?

This book lays the foundation of physical fitness in the form of multifunctional fitness, an exercise regime inspired by the rigorous, time-tested fitness programmes followed by armed forces all across the world. They are similar to each other in execution, barring a few changes that are observed over major armies of the world. Be it the US Navy Seals or US marines, the Special Air Services of the British army, or the special forces in the Indian army, the goal is common: To build a healthy, fit body, with stamina, strength and power, without getting bulging biceps or weightlifter muscles. This book intends to help achieve that aim by taking readers through various aspects of multifunctional fitness and all the peripheral inputs in the regime required to chart out a physical fitness programme for a beginner.

Functional Fitness: What, why and how

At the most basic level, functional fitness refers to exercises that improve daily activity. Every functional exercise challenges balance and coordination while simultaneously improving strength and range of motion. These are related to your daily requirements of performance and functions that you perform across the day. That is why it is called functional fitness. You would notice that army personnel across the world do not have bulging muscles, but they are tough. They can climb mountains, race up stairs, cross hurdles, climb ropes, get involved in close-quarters combat and hand-to-hand fight at any point of time. They can bear all weather conditions from –40 °C to upwards of 45 °C! They are always ready, and always fit.

Remaining fit for the everyday person is not a priority the way it is for armed forces personnel. They need to do it for a living, and being fighting fit at all times is a professional requirement. For those not in the army, therefore, there isn't a dire need to stay fit until an event comes up—like an upcoming sports event one wishes to participate in or a wedding where you want to show off a slim waistline, or simply, the new year and your new year resolution to become fitter!

But we sometimes get so singly focused on losing weight and toning up certain muscles that everything else takes a back seat. However, focusing only on one aspect of fitness or one part of your body and neglecting the others is neither good for your health nor a workout plan any instructor or fitness expert would ever approve of. So it is important that we shift our focus from training for events to training for everyday performance and function, making daily activities easier. With this goal in mind, we'll stay fit the whole year round, and sport that slim waistline or toned body every single day.

Let us now understand what the focus areas for attaining such fitness for life are.

1. Stability

Stability is the fundamental requirement of fitness. Without balance, one finds it difficult to perform simple everyday functions such as bending down to pick up an object, standing on your toes to reach for something overhead, running up a flight of stairs, getting out of the car, carrying things from Point A to Point B, etc.

Stability can be improved with exercises like single-leg balance exercises, lunges, jumping lunges, step-ups, lateral movements, posterior movements, agility drills and plyometrics. These exercises are done on stable ground during functional training to train your body to handle a heavier weight load—which means you're working at a higher intensity, burning more calories and developing more strength. There are also props like BOSU balls that add variety to a training routine and have their own benefits, but one should not depend on them alone for stability training.

2. *Strength*

All functional workouts should ideally be multi-joint workouts, and they must work the upper and lower body muscles in a balanced way so as to strengthen the entire body. In daily activities, we utilize our body as a whole, often without realizing it. Even though an activity may be more upper- or lower-body-dominant, we still rely on the other half for stability and support. Pushing a shopping cart, loading the groceries into the car, moving a gas cylinder, moving furniture at home are all examples of whole body activities. That is all that you need to have as your prime focus.

When you combine multiple muscle groups and exercise them in a synchronized manner, you are creating synergy in your body, and you see better results faster—greater stability, strength and power in *all* your muscles. Functional exercises also boost cardiovascular conditioning because your heart has to shuttle blood between the upper and lower body. And the neuromuscular system learns to fire more efficiently when you work several muscle groups at once, which leads to improved coordination and even stability. In this manner, we strengthen and augment our kinaesthetic intelligence.

3. Power

In fitness, power refers to the result of work done over short bursts of time. When you run up a flight of stairs, prevent yourself from falling, or reach to catch something before it falls, you are using power. Power exercises involve quick, explosive movements, like Olympic lifts, upper body plyometrics and lower body plyometrics. Exercises to develop power are performed over very short periods of time (say 20–60 seconds).

To move quickly and swiftly when action demands is the name of the game. Therefore, developing total body strength and power to perform daily chores is fundamental to functional fitness.

4. Multiplanar mobility

Our body is built to move in all directions: backwards, forwards, side to side, upwards and downwards. Dancing and skating are great examples of activities in which we move in different planes. The multifunctional fitness regimen incorporates exercises to achieve this multiplanar mobility with ease. Stretching and flexibility exercises are, therefore, an important part of a multifunctional exercise routine.

Software is more important than hardware

A person who goes to the gym and does not take a personal trainer usually follows a pattern of exercise that goes something like this: Walk/run on a treadmill and be at it for half an hour, then get on to a pumping iron type of machine and sweat it out, stretch for a bit, then use a few more of the various machines sitting around, and move on. This is a typical hardware-intensive workout programme.

Functional fitness uses lesser equipment and more body-weight-intensive exercises to achieve fitness goals, whatever they may be. In the way of equipment, there are ropes, medicine balls, roman rings and parallel bars, even logs and huge tyres, among a host of other things. Trainers play a crucial role in functional fitness; they guide you through your workout, correct your postures, etc., in real time so that you do the right set of exercises the right way. Trainers are the soul of a multifunctional fitness programme. If you have picked up this book, that's already an indication of your commitment to working out to become fit and healthy.

In this book, we have drawn a broad roadmap for you. Now you must chart out the exact path you wish to take.

Wish you a happy fitness journey. Best of luck!

1

Military Training and Its Components

'The purpose of training is to tighten up the slack, toughen the body, and polish the spirit.'

—MORIHEI UESHIBA, FOUNDER OF AIKIDO

EVERY NATION EXPECTS its armed forces to remain fighting fit 365 days of the year. The training of the armed forces, therefore, aims to prepare every single man and woman to face extreme battle conditions at a moment's notice. The ethos of physical fitness training across the armed forces is: The more you sweat in peace, the less you bleed in war.

Since it is the security of the nation that is at stake, the training methods have to be reliable, deliverable and time-tested. Therefore, the entire regimen is conceived and developed around the philosophy of fitness for life, of strength, endurance and stamina to face any condition anytime, anywhere.

If one examines any battlefield scenario, one realizes that the actions that a soldier would be required to perform are tough, complex and unpredictable in that they change as the situation changes. To top this, weather conditions are usually extreme: they can be extremely hot or extremely cold, high on rain and storms, and sometimes either too damp or too dry. Soldiers have to operate in mountains, deserts and jungles, each with a different terrain. A person has to be fit to survive all these harsh and myriad conditions. They should also be able to survive on rationed water and food for days without compromising what is expected of them.

Every soldier is expected, at all times during his service tenure, to be able to run for miles together with the weight of weapons, the ammunition kit as well as rations; negotiate complicated obstacles; rappel; scale a wall with ease, run up a mountain, do a cliff assault using ropes, and so on.

Therefore, functional fitness is a key element in achieving military physical fitness.

The armed forces usually have sprawling training centres where they train in the open with miles-long obstacle courses that help replicate an actual battlefield scenario. For indoor training, an individual is supposed to use his own body weight to do any number of exercises. Hence, the training is not highly dependent on machines and props; one's fitness programme can be implemented anywhere.

A person need not become a black cat commando or a marine; but anyone *can* become powerfully fit by using the exercises outlined in this book. You will be surprised at the transformation in your attitude, physical fitness and confidence that you will witness after following the functional fitness regimen. More importantly, you will achieve the 'fitness for life' attitude.

We would like to divide military training into three major components:

- Physical fitness/training to build stamina, endurance, strength and power;
- Negotiating and crossing actual obstacles that can be expected in a battlefield;
- Confidence-building so that a soldier does not flinch when he comes across a dangerous situation or an obstacle that seems to be impossible to cross or handle.

Let us see a few instances of these components, when applied.

Major components of physical training

Physical training (PT) is to lay down the foundation of a sound body and a sound mind. The entire focus is on building stamina, endurance, power and strength so that a soldier can then go and apply this in overcoming obstacle and building confidence. Some of the important ones are:

- *Running:* This is an individual effort to build stamina. One has to start running at a comfortable pace and gradually increase one's speed.
- *Calisthenics and dynamic exercises:* These are physical training tables defining a series of conditioning exercises that work all muscle groups at the same time.
- *Strength conditioning:* These exercises help build muscle strength in any body part that is focused upon. Rope climbing, using parallel bars, medicine ball,

and doing dips, and hanging knee raises are means to enable strength conditioning.

- *Rifle PT:* Rifles are a critical part of a soldier's uniform, especially in wartime, when it has to be on the soldier's person at all times. A rifle usually weighs 4–5 kg and the exercises are designed keeping in mind a soldier's requirement to carry his rifle wherever he goes. Training, therefore, ensures that carrying the rifle anywhere becomes effortless. Typical exercises in this category are fore up behind back, fore up back bend, fore up squat—all done at a moderate pace with cadence that can be gradually upped with time.
- *Log drill:* Log drills are team-conditioning exercises. They are excellent for developing strength and muscular endurance because they require the muscles to contract under heavy load. They also help develop teamwork and add variety to the PT programme.
- *Upper body development:* This is focused on building upper-body endurance and strength through a series of exercises like curls, rope and beam heaves, fireman lift and carry, triceps dips, crunches, and pull-ups.
- *Endurance training*: Exercise circuits are designed to develop and augment stamina, strength and endurance—the key requirement of military fitness. These circuits constitute a blend of running and executing exercises at designated stations in between. For example, a group has to run a cross-country marathon, and after a certain specific distance there is a workout point where the group does the specified exercises lasting a specific time period and continues to

run onwards to the next point. This is quite strenuous and builds overall endurance. These exercises could be squats, sprints, pull ups and mountain climbing-type obstacles/slopes.

Major components of obstacle course training

There are specially designed battle obstacle courses that prepare a soldier to negotiate different types of obstacles that he can encounter in a battlefield scenario. Some important ones are:

- Low hurdle is generally the first obstacle
- High hurdle and multiple hurdles: These are chest height
- Double ditch and 10-foot wall climb
- Monkey crawl on a rope with full battle kit
- *High balance:* This is a wooden structure where a soldier has to move from a lower height and run up to the upward climb and jump off at the end.
- *Cliff assault:* With a full battle kit and one's personal weapon, the soldier climbs a rope hanging from the top of the cliff using his legs—as support—and arms, in order to move up a wall-like cliff.
- *Low crawl:* A soldier has to crawl from under a barbed wire net using his elbows and legs, while keeping his head and buttocks down all the way.
- *Vaulting obstacle crossing:* There are a number of obstacles which have to be negotiated using different techniques.

- *Cargo net:* This obstacle looks simple but is not that easy to negotiate. It is like a spider net and you have to move up using your hands and feet, cross the bar on top and get down the other side.
- *Balance log:* These are logs placed at different heights and a soldier has to run on them. This exercise helps in learning how to focus on balancing your body on narrow strips.
- *Burma Bridge:* This is a bridge made of ropes and usually allows very little space for footwork. You hold the rope on both sides and walk on a single rope below.

Major components of confidence-building exercises

Negotiating dangerous obstacles is not easy and a soldier has to be trained to build his confidence so that he can overcome them fearlessly. A number of activities help build this spirit:

- *Confidence ladder climb:* Here, there is a very high ladder made of logs that one has to climb one step at a time. Once on the top, you cross over the log on the other side and climb down.
- *The weaver:* This comprises two inclined ladder-like structures with horizontal elements placed almost 1 m apart. One has to mount the first one, go under the second, go over the third, and so on until one reaches the top element. Then one climbs down on the other side.
- *Concertina barbed wire obstacle negotiation:* Here, a roll of concertina barbed wire is spread out and

soldiers have to throw a mat or a blanket on top of it, and then run up and roll over to cross this obstacle.

- *Tarzan swing:* Climb a high platform. A rope is attached several metres in front. Jump and catch the rope. Slide down until you touch the ground.
- *Confidence jump:* This is one of the most difficult exercises for those who are scared of heights. There are two towers in a water pool and a 1-foot-broad single plank platform connects the two. In the centre of this plank are three steps upwards and an extension and then three more steps downwards. A participant has to climb up the towers using either a rope or the ladder along the tower and walk on the plank, climb the three steps and then climb down the three other steps and cross over to the other tower. There he has to climb another few feet on the tower and reach a horizontal rope that is tied to the third tower. The person has to do a monkey crawl and come to the centre of the horizontal rope where there is a red flag. From the red flag, he has to jump down into the water. This is from a height of 60 feet, which is almost double of a 10-metre (32 feet) board in the swimming pool.

No-equipment workouts

No-equipment workouts involve PT tables which the soldier practise wherever he goes. As the name suggests, no equipment is needed.

Examples comprise doing double time in one place, punching horizontally as well as vertically, neck rotation and arm circling exercises, trunk and knee rotation exercises, triceps- and bicep-stretch, shoulder, neck and chest stretch exercises. Narrow and wide push-ups are done to retain strength. Hamstring stretch is for strengthening the back muscles in the thighs.

In a nutshell

- Armed forces constantly train their men and officers to keep them fit for the entire career. For a military man it is imperative that he remains fighting fit all the time because it is a professional obligation.
- The aim of military physical fitness training is to build an overall healthy and fit body with stamina, strength and power without building bulging biceps or multiple muscles across the body.
- In a battlefield scenario, the kind of functions that have to be performed by every man and woman is tough, complex and unpredictable. They have to do all of it amidst extremely harsh climates too.
- Every military operation does have a physical component to it. One has to negotiate obstacles, run for miles with weapons, among other things, sometimes live off the land with minimum rations, etc. Running up the hill, cliff assault and such tasks form a part of the fitness regimen. It is fitness for life.
- All these exercises are designed to ensure that one can perform functions deemed obligatory on the part of the soldier without getting exhausted. These are time-tested methods and have been used by armed forces across the world.

- We would like to divide armed forces training into three major components: (1) physical fitness/training to build stamina, endurance, strength, and power; (2) negotiating and crossing actual obstacles that can be expected in a battlefield; (3) confidence-building, so that a soldier doesn't flinch when he comes across a dangerous situation or an obstacle that seems to be impossible to handle.
- Physical training makes you fighting fit and ready to undertake the application part of battlefield training which involves overcoming different types of obstacles.
- Doing the obstacle crossing course several times pushes your confidence up several notches. And now you are ready to undertake the confidence course that has some seemingly impossible obstacles that require mental as well as physical endurance.

2

Self-evaluation and Formulating a Personal Fitness Plan

> 'What you get by achieving your goals is not as important as what you become by achieving your goals.'
>
> —ZIG ZIGLAR

TODAY, MOST PEOPLE are fitness conscious and willing to spend time and money to remain healthy and fit. But many of these aspirants have never done any systematic fitness training and others have done it intermittently. There are also those who have a sedentary lifestyle and some who have at least played some games and sports and whose body can take some amount of physical strain.

But whatever point your body's fitness level is at, take off from there. You have to decide for yourself what you actually want. Surprisingly, many people walk into a fitness studio and have no idea of what they want. Naturally then, the fitness instructor also cannot understand their requirements.

The foremost problem is that most people are not even aware of what their goals must comprise—what can be achieved and what cannot.

Fitness is also like ordering food at a restaurant. You need to have a menu in front of you and decide what all you would like to have.

In this chapter, we cover some of the most essential fitness items that will help you understand what all you can achieve with your fitness regimen. It will also help you assess your current health status.

After answering these questions you will know what you want and what you actually can achieve. Armed with this rough sketch, you can consult a trainer to help you fine-tune your requirements and draw up a workout chart alongside time-based goals depending on how much time you can afford to invest every day.

Remember, many people have the ability to pay for the gym but several of them take a membership and yet never use it; they lack the motivation and will to achieve this. And this is the most prominent cause for people to give up on a fitness programme.

Fitness History

1. When were you in the best shape of your life?

   ____

2. Have you been exercising consistently for the past 3 months?

   ____

3. When did you first start thinking about getting in shape?

____

4. On a scale of 1 to 10, how would you rate your present fitness level (1: worst–10: best)?

____

5. Are you satisfied with your current level of fitness?

____

6. Currently, how often do you participate in physical activity?
   - 5–7 times/week
   - 3–4 times/week
   - 1–2 times/week
   - not in the past 6 months

If active, list the activities you engage in.

____

____

____

____

____

____

____

____

____

____

Goal-setting

In order to increase your chances of being successful at achieving your goals, you need to first define your requirement.

Your goals must be SMART: Specific, Measurable, Attainable, Relevant and Time-calibrated.

S. Check against the goals you would like to accomplish. Here are some options to choose from:

- Reduce fat
- Tone muscles
- Improve sport-specific skills
- Improve flexibility
- Improve cardiovascular fitness
- Build muscle mass
- Improve exercise technique
- Build motivation and passion for fitness and achieving fitness target
- Improve overall health and well-being
- Imbibe better and healthier eating habits
- Pre/post-natal care rehabilitation
- Reduce stress
- Add variety to exercise regimen
- Build stamina
- Build overall strength
- Build power, speed, strength

- Build a chiselled body with abs
- Any other (please mention below)

____

____

M. You can monitor your progress on the following parameters:

- Body weight
- Girth measurements
- Fat testing through body reports
- Training log book
- Any others that you can think of

____

A. Activity frequency per week that you can afford to devote to your fitness regimen:

- 2 days
- 3–4 days
- 5 days or more

R. Make sure that this is something which is 'relevant' to you

Because Sally, my wife, has done an Iron Man which includes a 3.8 km swim followed by 180 km cycling and a 42 km run, I can't set the same target for myself as that's something relevant to her life goals, not mine.

T. All this has to be deadline oriented for you to be able to measure if you have achieved your goals.

1. What would an ideal exercise and work week look like for you? Please be as specific as possible. List your favourite classes, workouts, machines, activities, rest days, etc.

Day	Approximate Work Hours	Other Commitments	Ideal Time and Type of Exercise
Monday			
Tuesday			
Wednesday			
Thursday			
Friday			
Saturday			
Sunday			

2. What do you feel could slow your progress?
    - Lack of interest
    - Finding the exercise boring
    - Illness or injury

3. Please list in order of priority the fitness goals you would like to achieve in the next 3–12 months?

1. ____

2. ______________________________
3. ______________________________

4. How important is it for you to achieve these goals?
   - Very important
   - Important
   - Not very important

5. For how long have you been thinking of achieving these goals?

   ____

6. How will you feel once you've achieved these goals? Be specific.

   ____

   ____

   ____

   ____

   ____

   ____

7. Where do you place health in your life?
   - Low priority
   - Medium priority
   - High priority

8. What do you think is the most important thing your trainer can do to help you achieve your fitness goals?

____

____

____

____

____

9. Outline what you feel are the obstacles or your potential actions, behaviours, or activities that could impede your progress towards accomplishing your goals:

- Not training consistently
- Being lazy
- Upcoming vacation
- Busy season at work
- Not following the programme
- Allowing other responsibilities to become a priority over exercise
- Any other:

____

____

____

____

____

____

10. Outline three methods that you plan to use to overcome these obstacles:
    - ____________________
    - ____________________
    - ____________________

In a nutshell

- If you are planning to start an exercise schedule, you need to first know where you stand in terms of physical fitness. Do you play a few games, go for a run/walk once in a while or lead an absolutely sedentary life? This will be your take-off point.
- You then need to understand and decide what you want to achieve in terms of fitness. A whole lot of things can be done in terms of body fitness, but before you start training you must make a list of the things you want to achieve.
- These should be such that they should be realistic and doable. Your gym instructor can help you do that. This is called goal-setting.
- Now you need to define the number of hours you need to put in to achieve your defined goals. Thereafter, identify how many weeks/months you will give yourself to achieve your target at the pace you have set for yourself.
- Now you need to look into your motivation level and inspire yourself to keep at it come what may. Outline your strengths as well as weaknesses where your

workout regimen is concerned and then work on your weak points so that you keep yourself motivated to achieve your goals. For instance, if boredom is what puts you off, then try to do your exercises in a group. If you're feeling lazy, then you have to kick yourself into doing the activity every day. Once you have it going for a while, it will become a habit.

3

Functional Fitness Defined

'When it comes to eating right and exercising, there is no "I'll start tomorrow". Tomorrow is disease!'

—Terri Guillemets

Functional fitness is the latest buzz in the fitness industry—and not without reason. However, many people talk of functional fitness without actually knowing the concept and how it is different from regular fitness training.

The chief difference is that functional fitness is designed to make you fit instead of a bodybuilder. For many people, exercise is a way to maintain or improve their quality of life. And that's the focus of functional fitness.

We learnt in the first chapter the ethos and execution of a military fitness regimen. In a similar way, functional training helps you build strength, power and mobility that go beyond the gym. It is 'real world' fitness that helps you perform day-to-day functions without feeling tired or strained.

Importance of manual labour

About six to seven decades ago, people did a lot of manual labour. They had to walk miles to go to the market and bring heavy bags back home, again walking back the same distance. People constructed their own houses with wood and other assorted material. They had to cut trees with axes and carry logs on their heads and shoulders. Both these exercises would be extremely tiring. Menfolk had to load wood and other materials in hand carts and push them back home. Ploughing the fields was yet another tough task many people had to do. Women had to draw water from wells pulling our buckets full of water with the help of ropes tied to the buckets, and then carry those heavy vessels on their heads and shoulders back home. The wells would be located far away from their homes, on top of which weather conditions wouldn't always be congenial. The cycle was the order of the day and everyone cycled at least twenty to thirty miles or so a day including children. Horse-riding was another erstwhile mode of transport. It is, in fact, a means of good exercise for your legs, torso and lower back. Those of you who have done riding would realize that after a long ride, you are sweaty and tired. It's a wholesome exercise that works your core, quadriceps, hamstrings, glutes and Calves. Unfortunately, today most of us lead an absolute sedentary life and have access to motorized transport even in the remotest villages. While it brings comfort and efficiency, it makes us physically fragile.

As you read on, you will realize that most of the exercises listed in this book replicate or to some extent imitate what our ancestors did.

Functional training and physiotherapy

Physiotherapy emerged during the two major wars in the last century when the wounded soldiers who had lost some of their basic abilities, like walking, standing and bending, had to be rehabilitated. The therapy they received emphasized, among other things, core strength and mobility, which are essential for virtually all types of movement.

Over the decades, physical fitness became too focused on muscle and bodybuilding and relied on power lifting and machines, pushing the trainee towards a muscular physique. Consequently, the phase of improving real-life movements that are so important in our daily life was bypassed.

Taking a cue from physiotherapy, fitness ideology has renewed its focus on functional aspects, concentrating on multi-joint movements instead of single muscle group exercises. It also gives adequate weightage to building stamina and endurance required for our daily chores. To achieve this, it has expanded its equipment arsenal to include relatively recent innovations, like slosh pipes, battling ropes, sandbags, kettlebells and suspension trainers, along with more traditional tools like medicine balls, barbells and dumbbells. At the same time, they have done away with treadmills and other traditional machines, and reduced the emphasis on heavyweights.

In a way, it is back to basics.

Now, let us look at functional fitness in a little more detail before we graduate to chapters that will focus on specific exercises.

Unilateral and bilateral movement

Unilateral exercises focus on single-limb exercises. Bulgarian split squat is an example where you exercise the thigh and calf muscles of one leg at a time. Similarly, single-leg straight-leg dead lift is an example of unilateral exercise. Pistol squats is another example of unilateral movement. In the late 1990s, came along BOSU balls. They were adopted by functional fitness experts immediately. BOSU balls provide an uneven surface and thereby help in building stability and balance. Other props that can help achieve stability and balance can be balance discs or wobble boards. These exercises help strengthen the thigh and leg muscles. Since balance is important for all of us in daily life, this exercise is suitable for all. While on a cross-country run, you are treading an uneven ground and that requires a great amount of balance along with speed. In contrast, exercises like bench press, squats and box jumps exercise two limbs at a time (bilateral movement).

Functional training focuses on movements, not muscles

The traditional gym workouts focused on muscle-building exercises where the idea was to work on biceps, hamstrings or chest muscles. Most of the exercises involved one-plane motion known as 'sagittal' plane. But we seldom do activities confined to one plane in our daily life. In fact, we move in all three planes throughout the day. It must also be appreciated that any activity that we undertake does not engage or depend on only one muscle. Several muscles are in action; even when you climb stairs, for instance. That is how functional training identifies with the need of using multiple muscle groups at the same time and moving in all planes while performing our daily chores. An effective functional training programme also favours using free weights or one's own body weight over machines, focuses on working muscles through a full range of motion, and incorporates plenty of instability work.

What kind of training is right for you?

Functional fitness prepares your body muscles and joints to handle daily chores at home and office or even when engaging in some sports activity. Using muscles in the upper as well as lower body simultaneously, these exercises provide core stability and balance. For instance, squat is an exercise that trains and prepares muscles you use while you rise from a chair or sit down. The same muscle group and balance is required when you bend down to pick up an object from the ground. Those who play golf will realize that to get a ball out of the hole, which is half a foot deep, requires some effort and semblance of balance. Functional fitness exercises are designed to train and develop your muscles to make it easier and safer to perform everyday activities effortlessly.

Gyms use exercise tools such as fitness balls, kettlebells and weights in functional fitness workouts. If you want to do functional training at home, several exercises can be done without any equipment too.

If your aim is to be fit for carrying on with your day-to-day life effortlessly and that, without nursing tired or aching muscles, go for functional rather than conventional training.

Functional exercise training is especially beneficial as part of a comprehensive programme for older adults to improve balance, agility and muscle strength, and reduce the risk of falls, which becomes a big problem during old age. Instead of moving only the elbows, a functional exercise might involve the shoulders, spine, hips, knees and ankles. This type of training, when properly applied, can make everyday activities easier, reduce risk of injury and improve quality of life.

What may seem like simple activity, such as climbing steps, getting in and out of a car, or bending down to pick up an object, becomes difficult with old age and functional fitness can come to the rescue in such cases.

What are some examples of functional fitness exercises and add-on exercises that help augment fitness?

Yoga is one discipline that provides flexibility as well as muscle toning, augmenting the body's ability to withstand pressure, stretching and pulling. This is one of the finest workout methods that can be combined with functional training.

Multidirectional lunges help prepare your body for common activities, such as vacuuming and backyard work. To do a lunge, keep one leg in place and step out with the other leg—to the front, back or side—until your knee reaches a 90-degree angle and your rear knee is parallel to the floor.

Zumba, involving dance and aerobic movements performed to energetic music, can be fun as well as help in stamina building and balance. The choreography incorporates hip-hop, soca, samba, salsa, merengue and mambo. Squats and lunges are also included in it.

Can everyone undertake functional fitness exercises?

If you have been inactive for a while, are above 60 years of age, or are pregnant, it would be good to check with a doctor if you can engage in functional fitness exercises.

It's also a good idea to start with exercises that use only your own body weight for resistance. As you become more fit and, therefore, ready for more of a challenge, you can add more resistance in the form of weights. Working out under the water is a low-impact functional exercise because it puts less stress on the joints and the buoyancy of the water helps reduce the pressure on joints. Water also acts as a form of resistance, so strength exercises can be performed in the water without heavy weights.

Return on your investment with functional training

Starting a fitness programme may be one of the best things you can do for your health and well-being. Physical activity can reduce risks of chronic disease, improve your balance and coordination, help you lose weight, increase your metabolism and even boost your self-esteem. And you can reap these benefits regardless of your age, gender or physical ability.

Here are some specific gains that can be guaranteed:

1. Boosts energy

As you exercise, your heart pumps faster and you take in more fresh air, and the body gets energized. Your cardiovascular system and lungs start working more efficiently and become stronger. You don't gasp for breath when climbing stairs or walking briskly. Exercise allows for oxygen and optimizes your metabolism to digest better and delivers nutrients to your tissues and muscles. Most importantly, it induces in you that feel-good factor and you feel stronger, lighter and happier.

2. Allows for sound sleep

This is something we all look forward to. Sleep deprivation is the biggest health hazard today. People lead a sedentary life: after being glued to the desk for almost 12 hours a day, you drive back home, have dinner and hit the bed. Naturally, the body is just not tired enough to sleep. Crazy office hours and frequent travelling take their own toll. Exercising helps the body tire out, therefore enabling better, deeper, more energizing sleep. But one should not exercise right before bedtime because it can over-energize your body, and make you active and unable to hit the sack.

3. Lifts your mood

If you have had a tough day, hit the gym for 45 minutes or take a brisk walk or jog and you will feel relaxed after that. When you exercise, your body releases chemicals called endorphins. These endorphins interact with the receptors in your brain that reduce your perception of pain. Endorphins also trigger a positive feeling in the body, similar to that of morphine. Exercise definitely impacts your physique positively and that, in turn, boosts your self-esteem and confidence.

4. *Fights disease and builds immunity*

Being active boosts high-density lipoprotein (HDL), the good cholesterol, and reduces unhealthy triglycerides. This decreases the risk of heart disease. Regular exercise helps you in so many ways. It reduces the risk of strokes, high blood pressure, type-2 diabetes, metabolic syndrome and even arthritis.

5. *Helps you shed weight*

If you exercise regularly and consistently, and watch your diet a bit, you are bound to lose flab around your stomach and thighs and improve your BMI. BMI, or body mass index, is a ratio of your weight to your height, age and gender. It is an approximate measure of whether someone is over- or underweight, calculated by dividing their weight in kilograms by the square of their height in metres.

The days you can't hit the gym, make it a point to go and take a long brisk walk or jog. Do some basic exercises like sit-ups and push-ups, so that there is no major break in your exercising routine. Consistency is the key to success. You can't skip five days in week and then expect visible results.

6. *Is fun and helps you socialize*

Exercise and physical activity can be made enjoyable, especially when done in a group. It gives you a chance to unwind, speak to others, enjoy the outdoors or get charged up. Physical activity can also help you connect with family or friends in a fun social setting.

So, take a yoga class, hit the hiking trails, go for a cycling trip or get a swimming pool membership. Find a physical activity you enjoy, and just do it. If you get bored, there are so many things you can do to fight that.

7. Is also great for women

A lot of women are scared of lifting weights and getting into fitness because they want a toned body but not bulging, manly muscles. The toned body that most women dream of will not happen doing 30-minute treadmill runs, but through good weight training and functional training.

What is the optimum physical fitness activity?

There is no 'one size fits all' kind of schedule when it comes to working out, but for starters, we recommend the following:

- If you haven't exercised for a long time, have chronic health problems, such as heart disease, diabetes or arthritis, or any other concerns, it is good to check with your doctor before planning your exercise regimen.
- Consider your fitness goals and what you want to achieve and how much time you can invest in a week before you start designing your fitness programme. Your gym instructor will also ask you these questions as you move along.
- Aim for at least 150 minutes per week of moderate intensity exercise, or 75 minutes per week of vigorous exercise to start with. One week has 10,080 minutes and you can remain fit by working out for just 1.5 per cent of that time!
- Whatever time you spend, it must be judiciously spent, i.e., you must allocate time for different

kinds of exercises. Try to engage in a combination of vigorous and moderate aerobic exercises, such as walking, running or swimming. Squeeze in strength training at least twice per week by lifting free weights, using weight machines or doing body weight exercises.

- Spread out your activities throughout the week. If you want to lose weight or meet specific fitness goals, you may need to ramp up your exercise efforts.
- Everybody doesn't like all types of exercises and there are alternatives available. Therefore, consider your likes and dislikes and appreciate your barriers and limitations so that you don't bite more than you can chew. This becomes extremely important for a novice or a beginner because too steep a goal coupled with exercises you are not comfortable with can make you averse to this entire activity.

Remember, you should first get hooked to this new activity and only then shift gears to add to the degree of difficulty—but gradually. You are looking at altering your lifestyle and, therefore, it should be good, something you like. By planning carefully and pacing your workout schedule, you can make fitness a healthy habit that lasts a lifetime.

Brief overview of your functional fitness exercises

Broadly speaking, there are three areas to look at. They are stretching, aerobics and strength building. Let us look at each one of them briefly. This will help you understand the other chapters in the book.

Stretching and flexibility

This is extremely important for any fitness programme or sports activity. Even when you play a game as relaxed as golf, you need to warm up a bit and stretch your back muscles, arms and legs before you take your first shot at the tee. When it comes to more strenuous and demanding sports activity, it becomes even more imperative to stretch before hitting the ground. You won't see a professional footballer or cricketer, getting on the playing field without stretching or warming up. We need to understand that it's not only Pro-s who need to do this; any of us participating in a sports activity needs to warm up and stretch our muscles. This helps protect our muscles from getting damaged or overstretched as we start the game. It also augments body flexibility.

It is also important to cool down gradually after a workout. Strength training and aerobic exercises cause muscles to contract and tighten. Light stretching exercises after a workout help loosen up muscles and joints, and boost circulation.

It is a good idea to do a bit of warm-up and stretching on the day you are not exercising. This lets you maintain flexibility. In all the cases above, warm-up and stretching must be gentle and light, never vigorous. Hold each stretch for 30–40 seconds and breathe freely. You can expect a bit of tension while stretching (and that is the purpose) but it should not cause too much pain. Pain means you are overstretching that muscle or muscle group.

Strength training

With a regular strength-building programme, you can reduce body fat. It also helps build stronger bones and increases your lean muscle mass. It further helps burn calories. Three to five sets of 12–15 repetitions of strength exercises of all the major muscle groups performed at least two times a week is sufficient to maintain muscle mass. You can do these at the gym or even at home without any equipment. Gyms have machines and free weights that provide several exercising options. At home, you may use your own body weight for this purpose.

Aerobics

'Aerobic' stands for exercise taken to improve the efficiency of the body's cardiovascular system in absorbing and transporting oxygen. In military training, aerobics plays a very important part because it trains a soldier to walk or run over very long distances without getting breathless.

For a healthy person, an investment of 75 minutes of vigorous exercises or 150 minutes of moderate exercise a week is desirable. You don't have to do all this in one shot. It can be spread over a week. For instance five days of a 30-minute walk is good enough and meets the criterion of 150 minutes in a week. Walking is one of the most natural forms of exercise. It's safe, it's simple, and all it takes to get started is a good pair of walking shoes and a commitment to include aerobic exercise in your daily routine. Other aerobic exercises such as jogging, swimming or cycling or indoor cycling are variations that can prove useful.

In a nutshell

- Functional fitness prepares a person for doing his daily chores without getting tired. It prepares you to become real-life-worthy.

- The idea of fitness training today is to counter the sedentary lifestyle most of us lead. Earlier, people had to do physical labour because every activity had to be performed without any automated help. People climbed steps as there were no lifts; they walked or cycled for miles to reach their place of work. Menfolk cut wood, loaded it into hand carts and towed them for miles. Today, most people feel incapable of carrying even their shopping bags from the mall to their cars and you also see them huffing and puffing when climbing steps.
- Physiotherapy evolved during the two major world wars in the last century where many injured soldiers lost basic functions, like walking. Modern physiotherapy is to a large extent, a derivative of yoga. Such medical advancement was also a motivational input to develop functional fitness.
- Functional training emphasizes unilateral and bilateral movement, and also focuses more on movement than muscle.
- Functional fitness exercises provide several benefits. It helps shed weight, get sound sleep, boost energy, build immunity, uplift one's mood and even aids in socializing.
- This is the best bet for women who want to tone their bodies and look fighting fit. It targets aerobics, strength-building and flexibility.

4

Fitness Fundas: Components of Body Fitness

> 'I fear not the man who has practised 10000 kicks once, but I fear the man who has practised one kick 10000 times.'
>
> —BRUCE LEE

FOR MOST PEOPLE it will be difficult to correctly explain what constitutes a healthy and fit body. Some would say a fit person needs to have strength, some may say stamina and some may say six-pack abs or a body with big biceps. None of these answers are actually wrong, but they are not all-encompassing. Therefore, we need to look at a healthy and fit body more holistically. If you are going to get into fitness training, you must know what is to be achieved and understand the parameters of being fit.

Can we define certain parameters, which, if put together, could define a fit and a healthy body? Yes, we can. Several experts segregate such parameters and make a list of these. These lists differ a little but most cover all that is required. In addition, nomenclatures may also differ slightly.

In the context of functional fitness, these parameters are very important as each one has its own role to play. Functional training is like 'work fitness training'. It is for those who are living in semi-urban or urban areas where life, although relatively comfortable than the kind that's led by a villager, has its own stressors. We call them 'urban soldiers'—who need to carry a haversack bag with a laptop, something to eat, a water bottle and some notebooks or reading material. Salespersons also carry samples of whatever they are trying to sell. For them to lug around so much on their shoulders for a few hours can be tiring. These are the people who may have to change a tyre once in a while, carry suitcases from their flat to the car and load them. They may sometimes have to move some furniture at home or lift and move a 15 kg gas cylinder.

If a healthy and fit body needs to be benchmarked against some parameters and viewed as a collection of certain attributes, we would like to use *seven* such attributes or components of body fitness. These attributes are in the context of functional fitness.

All our training exercises and regimes as well as schedules described in this book cater to all these fitness components.

Power

To those who are uninitiated, power, strength and endurance look like country cousins—they appear to be similar, if not the same. But there is a difference.

Power has a lot to do with speed. The ability to generate force as quickly as possible is known as power. For example, the speed with which a batsman swings his bat in cricket denotes power.

In physics, power is the amount of energy transferred per unit of time. The fitness definition of power is also on the same lines. Time is central to it and the definition of speed in science is: Speed is the rate at which an object covers distance.

Strength

It is the ability of a muscle or the body to generate as much possible force without time as an important factor. Strength can be further divided into three components:

- *Muscular strength with respect to maximum load bearing:* This is pulling or pushing a maximum load just once. For example, in bench press, a person who can do a bench press with a 200 kg weight has more muscular strength than the one who cannot go beyond 150 kg.
- *Muscular strength with respect to muscular contraction:* This is like testing the strength of someone's grip; for example, how much strength he can use to squeeze your hand and hold it for as long as possible. To measure this, give two individuals a set of grippers each and tell them to squeeze them fully and hold them there—check for how long they can hold them. The one who can hold out longer has more muscle contraction strength.
- *Muscular strength with respect to endurance:* Endure means 'to suffer'. Endurance is the ability to tolerate

stress or strain. For example, a person who has gone through five surgeries has endured more than a person who has gone through the same surgery three times. In the context of fitness, it indicates your capacity to endure a challenging fitness, the number of times you can engage in a single fitness activity. A hundred push-ups denote more endurance than seventy-five. The same goes for any weight exercise. How many reps (repetitions) can you do with a sub-maximal load?

Strength training helps build all the above attributes in a person holistically.

When the co-author (Sally Jones) was training for the Ironman Triathlon, her transition from a 90-km cycling capacity to a 180-km cycling capacity took a lot on her body as building this takes a lot of time and effort. The point is that we all have some inbuilt endurance and it takes time and consistent effort to increase it.

What gets even more intense is endurance training in the military as it adds another dimension to endurance with a heavy backpack and a weapon on your shoulder for a long distance. Endurance runs start at 3.2 km and go on to 16 km, 26 km, 36 km and finally a 40-km non-stop run.

Let us now compare strength with power in scientific terms.

1. Power clean

To execute a clean, a lifter grasps the barbell just outside the legs, typically using a hook grip. Once the barbell is above the knees, the lifter extends explosively, raising the bar as high as possible before quickly dropping into a squat and receiving it in a 'racked' position in front of the neck and resting on the shoulders.

Strength generated = Mass × Distance

Say the weight of the barbell was 100 kg. If he moves the weight to a height of 6 feet, then the strength is

100 kg × 6 ft = 600 units

Power is the amount of work per unit of time, and the power clean takes just 1 second; so power is

600 work units/1 second = 600 units

2. *Bench press*

Suppose a person takes 2 seconds to perform a bench press with 100 kg, and the weights are lifted to a height of 3 feet.

Since strength generated = Mass × Distance

Work (strength) = 100 × 3 = 300 units

Power = work/time = 300/2 = 150 units

In example (a), the power generated is more because of less time taken for this movement. In example (b), the power is less than the work because it took longer. Therefore, power exercises will have more power units than strength exercises.

Stamina

According to the dictionary, stamina means endurance, staying power, indefatigability, tirelessness, resistance, resilience, fortitude, strength, vigour, energy, staunchness, steadfastness, robustness, toughness, determination, tenacity, perseverance.

In terms of fitness, it is the ability to sustain prolonged physical effort. Duration matters in stamina. For instance, can you cycle 30 km non-stop? If you can, but another person can do 40 km, then he has more stamina than you do. Can you play five sets of tennis at a stretch? Can you play six games of squash without taking a break? All these are indicators of stamina.

Muscles are like engines that run on fuel. While automobiles burn petrol or diesel, our muscles burn fat and carbohydrates. Oxygen plays a key role in this because it is used to burn fat and carbohydrates for fuel to keep our engines running. The more efficient our muscles are at consuming oxygen, the more fuel we can burn, the more fit we are, and we can exercise longer.

Stamina involves both *aerobic endurance*, which is prolonged, low-to-moderate intensity exercise (such as jogging for several kilometres in one go), and *anaerobic endurance*, which is short and very intense exercise (such as short bursts of sprints, skipping, or on-the-spot quick running).

Aerobic exercises are also known as cardio exercises in gym lingo—exercises that require pumping of oxygenated blood by the heart to deliver oxygen to working muscles. Aerobic exercise stimulates the heart rate and breathing rate in a way that can be sustained for the exercise session. Examples of aerobic exercises include cardio machines, looping (indoor cycling), running, swimming, walking, hiking, dancing, cross-country skiing and kick-boxing.

In contrast, anaerobic exercise is activity that causes you to run out of breath fast, like when you lift weights for improving strength, when you sprint, or when you climb a long flight of stairs.

The best way to increase your stamina is with exercises that challenge both types of endurance and muscles. You need to exert your body, and the ultimate aim should be to reach your peak performance as far as stamina is concerned.

Stamina is a requirement not only for athletes and sportspersons, but for everyone.

Stamina is also linked to endurance. Endurance is something that lets you face exertion for a longer period, and stamina includes the energy levels and overall health that boost one's endurance.

To boost your stamina you need to get in shape, which means augmenting your lung capacity, bettering your metabolism and strengthening your body and heart muscles. You need to start slowly and build up stamina gradually. Never overexert yourself, but go slow till your body has adapted to a more vigorous exercise regimen. Overexertion can be harmful and dangerous, and after the age of 40, it can create cardiac complications. Consulting a doctor before you venture out is a good idea. This is highly recommended for people who have lived a sedentary life for a very long time and one fine day decide to build stamina. Remember, Rome was not built in a day. The same is applicable to building your stamina and overall fit body.

One can start with walking, which is the best exercise for all age groups. Then increase the pace and distance—but gradually. Then start cycling, rowing, jogging and playing light outdoor games. Then try long treks and marathon walks.

Devoting 30 minutes to exercising daily is must. According to the American Heart Association, we need a minimum of 150 minutes of exercise per week.

One cardinal principle for doing any exercise is that it must be preceded by a proper warm-up exercise. After the exercise, a cooling down period must also be provided for. This also prevents any muscle strain or injury.

With regular and high-intensity workouts, your stamina and endurance are sure to increase.

Agility

One simple definition of agility is the ability to change the body's position efficiently and quickly, and it requires a combination of skills like balance, coordination, speed, reflexes, strength and endurance.

Balance means maintaining equilibrium while standing as well as moving. Coordination means how you connect your body movements with sensory perception that happens through senses like hearing, vision and touch. At the beginning of a race, when a shot is fired, athletes have to sprint. Even a millisecond can make the difference between a winner and a loser. Again, a fielder's catching a ball requires tremendous coordination. Speed is the ability to move the body quickly. Dynamic balance, for example, is a cricketer running while looking up and trying to catch the ball. Strength is related to muscle groups having sufficient ability to overcome any impediment or resistance to motion or even a static posture.

In fitness and physical activity, agility is often defined in terms of an individual sport, due to it being an integration of many components, each used differently, specific to different sports. Sheppard and Young define agility as a 'rapid whole body movement with change of velocity or direction in response to a stimulus'. The key words in this definition are 'rapid' and 'in response to a stimulus'. Now these are important points to build on. Earlier, the measure of agility was the ability of rapidly changing direction multiple times. But it fell short as far as daily chores and sports were concerned.

Let us take boxing as an example. The two boxers are quick on their feet and try to avoid a punch by the opponent by ducking or using their arms to block the punch. The stimulus is the opponent's punch.

In cricket, a batsman faces a ball coming at him at a speed of 160 km/hr and the ball spins as it hits the ground. The batsman uses his visual capability to decide how to play the shot. He moves either a step forward or a step back accordingly to take a shot. Look at a pilot flying at 2 Mach speed and he has to turn very quickly during a dog fight in battle. The reaction time is just a split second. Therefore, your reflexes are related to your agility. (Here, mental agility and physical movement may be minimal with the joystick and the foot control, but are nevertheless very critical.)

In group sports like football, rugby or hockey, agility is very important. In basketball, a player is dribbling the ball and the others are trying to stop him. Observe how quickly he changes his position, moves the ball, coordinating his escape every time someone tries to stop him. In football, the goalkeeper too has to be very agile because he doesn't know from which side the ball will come. Watch how tense a goalkeeper is during a penalty shot, he has to react to the body language of the striker and also lunge quickly to block the ball.

The complexity of our body movement relates to reaction time, response time, perception, judgement and anticipation.

When a racing car driver drives at 300 km/hour, it is his judgement and anticipation that count for his survival. Obviously he looks in the rear mirror, keeping a track of his opponents on the left and the right and also watches the tunnel he will reach in a few seconds and accordingly handles his paddle, brakes and gears.

Now imagine someone throwing a stone at you. You can save a skull fracture if you can quickly react and duck down. Our eyes are quicker and that is why, many times a person gets hurt but manages to save his eye. This is the reflex action which is related to agility.

Speaking of sensory perception, note how the moment your arm touches a hot iron, you instantly jump away (reflex action and your agility). Our bodies have this ability to save us from injuries.

Therefore, agility is one of the most important aspects of our daily lives; it is also an important component in sports.

It is essential, therefore, to build agility in your fitness training. One can create some innovative exercises that can improve one's agility.

Some of the exercises, although appearing simple, are great to build overall agility:

Horizontal ladder exercises

A horizontal ladder is required here, and you move through each square raising your leg, thigh parallel to ground, and move step by step till you reach the other end. You can innovatively use this to do scissors. For upper body toning, drop to a hands-down position and move through the ladder.

Agility balls

These are balls that bounce in different directions on impact with the wall or floor. You can ask a partner to throw and catch, or chuck it across a wall to catch it back as it bounces off in a different direction.

Low hurdles

These are hurdles about 12 inches high. Alternatively, you can use low boxes and arrange them horizontally. Have at least ten of them. You can use various combinations to jump and cross a hurdle and then pause and move to the next one till you finish all ten. Or you may cross over one and come back to the first and then move to cross over two of them at the same time and again come back and then do three, and so on. This can be tricky and tiring. By using different combinations, you can make it as interesting as possible.

Medicine ball throws

As you would with a small agility ball, try this with a midsized medicine ball that you can handle. Stand a short distance from a wall and throw the ball at it in such a way that it rebounds slightly to the right. You move a step to the right and catch the ball. Do this ten times and then reverse the direction to the left. You can make it difficult by squatting and lunging to get the ball back in your hands as you move along.

Stability

You need to be stable while walking, running, running up the stairs, crossing an obstacle, or while standing still. This is a basic requirement for all human beings and not specific to an athlete or a soldier.

As kids, we ran around trees, swung from monkey bars, and balanced on merry-go-rounds. One-legged, three-legged, and sack races were designed for fun, but were great exercises to achieve stability. All these inadvertently promoted and brought stability into our system. As we grew, we stopped doing all this and are now happy with sitting or lying down for almost the entire day.

The biggest culprit behind our losing our ability to remain stable is our sedentary lifestyle where we remain seated for long hours in schools, colleges and our workplace and don't move much in twenty-four hours. Your hip and leg muscles don't get enough stretch and the body doesn't get a chance to make its effort to trigger stability because you are sitting in a stable, comfortable position almost all the time.

It does not require too much time or effort to get this ability activated. Just five to ten minutes in your fitness schedule a day would be enough. Stability is a must for boxers, fencing players, kick-boxers, and those trained in martial arts such as kung fu. In fact, in karate, the stances (your feet apart) are such that you are firmly set on the ground so that the opponent cannot destabilize you.

Building stability

A proprioceptively enriched environment needs to be set up for exercises that induce stability; in simple words, this means to work out in an unstable (yet controllable) physical situation in which exercises that cause the body to use its internal balance and stabilization mechanisms are performed.

There can be a number of simple exercises that can be added to your fitness programme to enhance stability.

a. Simple standing balance on one leg

Here, you should stand erect on a single leg and try to balance your body. You bend your other leg backwards and raise it at a 90 degree-angle, bringing the part of the leg below the knee parallel to the ground. Hold for 10 to 20 seconds and bring it down. Repeat with the other leg now. Do this with each leg 10 to 12 times.

b. Single leg reach

Here, you reach down to the standing leg's foot. Keep your standing leg a little bent so that you don't overstrain your muscle.

Other variations with simple props

You can use a BOSU ball and stand on it to stay stable for a short period, say 10 seconds, and then increase the duration. A parallel beam at a height of 4 feet is also very helpful. Mount and walk on this, very slowly at first, and then you can repeat it at a faster pace as you continue to improve your balance. Initially, you can also spread your arms on the sides parallel to the ground for better balance and then you can do it with your arms by your sides. There can be a number of variations to this. The idea of such exercises is to make your balancing faculty sharper.

Flexibility

How much range of motion you have around your joints and muscles is one measure of flexibility. It also refers to the mobility and stretch ability of your muscles, which allows for more movement around the joints. Range of motion is the distance your joints can cover and the direction they can take, while mobility is the ability to move without restriction. Put together, they define and determine how supple your body is.

A stiff body is prone to injuries and also not very amenable to doing physical exercises.

Even dancers, athletes and sportspersons need a flexible body. During your day-to-day activities, it makes bending, walking and lifting easier. Since flexibility is the range of motion around a joint, good flexibility in the joints can help prevent injuries through all stages of life. If you want to improve your flexibility, try activities that lengthen the muscles and stretch your body, such as swimming or a basic stretching programme.

Importance of flexibility training

As you train for agility, stamina and stability, it is also essential to go for some exercises that make your body less rigid and more flexible. When your muscles are flexible, you are less likely to get injured during physical activity. Flexibility training can help reduce muscle soreness post-workout. When you do stretching exercises after a workout, it loosens the muscles and makes them more relaxed.

It also helps improve your overall performance because when joints and muscles are flexible, you need less energy for any body movement.

Basic activities for keeping your body supple and flexible

Often, while designing a fitness programme, people miss the aspect of flexibility. In fact, it is one of the most effective and important parts of fitness. One of the major achievements of yoga is to make a body flexible, limber and nimble. It makes for better and graceful movement of the body in every activity.

Here are some important points to keep in mind while practising stretching:

- Stretch your entire body because both the upper and lower parts of the body are important.
- Warm up a little before attempting the stretching exercises.
- Hold your stretched position for 20–30 seconds.
- Stretch to the point where there is a slight tautness and mild tension. Never overstretch, as this can cause serious injury. Flexibility like any other ability has to be built gradually.
- Breathe normally while stretching.

Best way to improve flexibility

Activities such as yoga and Pilates can help stretch and strengthen your muscles, tendons and ligaments, in addition to improving your range of motion.

Yoga, a five thousand-year-old technique which has its roots in the eastern beliefs such as Buddhism and Hinduism, has been internationally recognized for its contribution to improving flexibility. Pilates, a technique developed by Joseph Pilates in the early 1900s, is also referred to as 'contrology' as it emphasizes controlled movement of body parts, muscles and joints. This is also gaining popularity in Western countries. Joseph Pilates believed that there was a relation between body and mind fitness, and his methods addressed both. It is based on nine principles. These are concentration, control, centring, flow, postural alignment, precision, stamina and relaxation.

Both yoga and Pilates offer stress relief, flexibility, strength, control and endurance. The biggest difference between the two is the emphasis on the spiritual component; yoga also looks at spiritual experience, whereas Pilates does not.

Yoga is often used as a form of meditation. It is meant to bring the user a sense of inner peace and calm. Pilates, in contrast, was developed with the idea of helping the user attain mental and physical toughness, as well as a connection between the two. Yoga utilizes this as well, but also introduces a spirituality concept. Yoga classes, therefore, tend to be more serene and quiet, with a soft-spoken instructor guiding you along the way. Pilates, on the other hand, can range from quiet and peaceful to tough and intense.

In a way, Pilates can be viewed as a subset of yoga or even a derivative so to say. Pilates makes use of some equipment while technically and classically, yoga uses no equipment at all. However, now some people teaching modern yoga have started introducing some equipment to make it more modern in outlook and also more acceptable to a younger audience.

Yoga is based on the idea of centring and flexibility, while Pilates was developed as an all-around body conditioning programme, especially meant to help wounded war veterans supplement their rehab. This distinction is fundamental to the rest of the differences between the two. Pilates has a close resemblance to functional fitness as this also emerged from making wounded soldiers self-sufficient, helping them in performing their daily chores with ease.

Pilates offers participants the chance to be a bit more social and offers a more motivational approach than yoga may provide, while yoga can be a kind of escape, giving one a chance to realign oneself.

Endurance

The word endurance was used earlier in this chapter in the context of stamina. In fact, endurance and stamina are like country cousins. We will now look at endurance in little more detail.

Sometimes you may wonder why you are unable to keep up with a sport or activity of your choice for a longer period than others. It may happen that someone can climb four storeys of a building faster than his friends and still not be out of breath. This difference has to do with one's endurance.

The simplest definition of endurance is that it is the ability to sustain a physical activity for a prolonged period of time.

A long-distance runner or a person running a 1500-metre race requires a higher level of endurance than a sprinter who runs a 100-metre dash. Sustainability over a period of time is of essence. A person with a higher level of endurance has a lower resting heart rate because his heart is more efficient. Such people also have stronger and more efficient muscles that can take an onslaught of physical activity more effectively.

Endurance is of two types: aerobic and muscular. Let us look at both of them.

Aerobic endurance

As mentioned before, aerobic means relating to or requiring oxygen, and refers to the use of oxygen to adequately meet the body's energy demands during exercise via aerobic metabolism. Exercises and activities are cardiovascular in nature, like running long distances, jogging, swimming and cycling.

Long-distance running, cycling and swimming are the activities included in triathlons. The Ironman Triathlon is one of a series of long-distance triathlon races organized by the World Triathlon Corporation, consisting of a 3.86 km swim, a 180.25 km bicycle ride and a 42.20 km marathon run, raced in that order and without a break! It is considered one of the most difficult one-day sporting events in the world.

Ironman events have a limited time of 17 hours to complete the race. All three events are back to back. The mandatory cut-off time for the 3.86 km swim is 2 hours 20 minutes, the mandatory cut-off time for the 180 km cycle is 8 hours 10 minutes, and the mandatory cut-off time for the marathon is 6 hours 30 minutes. Any participant who manages to complete the triathlon within these time constraints is designated an Ironman.

Muscular endurance

The ability to perform several repetitions against resistance for a prolonged period is the measure of muscular endurance. Strength and endurance put together result in muscular endurance. In addition to aerobic or cardio endurance, muscular endurance is critical for sports activities like hockey, football, cricket and also long-distance events like marathon, cycling and swimming. You may have cardio sustainability, but if your muscles don't hold out, you will not be able to do well in these sports or any physical activity for that matter.

For people who want to remain fit and are not into sports as such, there is no need to go for specific endurance building programmes. This differs for athletes and sportspersons who want to excel at their particular sport or event. Any type of training in that case must replicate the demands of that sport. For resistance training or muscular endurance, the load used during the training must match the load or resistance encountered during that sports activity. The number of repetitions must match or be a little more than that required during a real event. For instance, if a boxing bout is for say 3 minutes, then the training must ensure that you last for a little longer than that.

Muscular endurance can be long-term or short-term, depending on the event one is preparing for.

Long-term muscular endurance is required for events that last more than two or three minutes, like rowing, triathlons, marathons or a 5000-metre race. The time period here is longer and loads, a little lighter, so that the activity can be performed for a longer period of time without muscles getting fatigued. To mimic this in the gym space you need to ensure that the equipment you would use are close to each other so that the rest period is minimum between sets of exercise.

Short-term muscular endurance is advantageous when an athlete is participating in events/sports that require effort for time spans ranging between 30 seconds and 2 minutes. A 100-metre sprint requires less than 12 seconds, and an 800-metre run less than 2 minutes. Power sports like football, fencing and boxing require tremendous energy to be delivered in a short time and in spurts.

Simple ways to improve your aerobic endurance

You should start with some activity of your choice and start with the level which you are comfortable at. Don't strain yourself. Do this for a period of time and then keep adding a few minutes a week to get your body used to doing this activity for longer durations. For instance, you may start your endurance fitness programme with walking, doing a 30-minute circuit at your nearest park. After a week, do this for 35 minutes and keep increasing the duration till you are able to clock 1 hour. At this point, you can count the number of rounds you take of the park in 1 hour. Thereafter, you may like to make your walk more brisk so as to increase your speed and reduce the time taken to complete the number of rounds or, in other words, do more rounds in 1 hour.

You could also try interval training where you alternate between hard and light activity. You could build this into your walking schedule where you walk for 10 minutes and then jog for 5, alternately. This way you will build endurance gradually and within a few weeks see the change for yourself. You will be able to sustain continuous physical activity for a longer time with less fatigue.

Some simple aerobic endurance exercises are given below:

- Brisk walks
- Running/jogging
- Dancing
- Swimming

- Biking
- Stair climbing
- Playing sports such as tennis, basketball, soccer or squash

How much do you require?

Anyone who wants to be qualified as a physically fit person must build endurance as a part of his or her exercise routine. Building endurance helps you to perform your daily chores with ease. People who want to start a fitness programme, having led a sedentary life, manning a desk twelve hours a day, must never rush. Work your way up slowly. Adults must get a two-and-a-half hour physical activity (moderate to intense) per week. This is the minimum required to remain fit—150 minutes spread over a week or 5 days comes to only 30 minutes a day. But this is the bare minimum to start with and is surely achievable. It is good to go slow and set realistic goals so that you do not give up and sustain this healthy habit—to endure the endurance.

In a nutshell

- Before one starts a fitness programme, it is essential to understand what a healthy and fit body is. Strength, stamina or bulging muscles? One needs to look at fitness more holistically.
- There are seven attributes/parameters that can holistically describe fitness or a fit body.
- Functional fitness is like 'work fitness'. It is for those who are doing any job for living in semi-urban or

urban areas where life is relatively comfortable and easy. These 'urban soldiers' who need to carry at most a haversack bag with a laptop, something to eat, a water bottle and some notebooks or reading material have to be up and about for 10–12 hours a day.

- Power is the first thing one thinks of when we talk of fitness. Power has to do with speed, the ability to generate as much force as quickly as possible.
- Strength is the ability of a muscle or the body to generate force—as much as possible—with no concern for time it takes.
- In fitness terms, stamina is the ability to sustain prolonged physical effort.
- Agility is the ability to change the body's position efficiently, and requires the combination of skills like balance, coordination, speed, reflexes, strength and endurance.
- Stability is a basic requirement for all human beings and not specific to an athlete or a combatant soldier.
- Flexibility refers to the range of motion you have around your joints and muscles. It also refers to the mobility and stretch ability of your muscles, which allows for greater and smoother movement.
- Endurance is the ability to sustain a physical strain for a prolonged period of time.

5

Basic Blocks of Functional Training

'We do not stop exercising because we grow old—we grow old because we stop exercising.'

—Dr Kenneth Cooper

Before we start with functional training exercises, it is essential to understand the types or modalities of functional training. The best part of functional training is that first, it replicates real-life scenarios and helps you live your life more effectively and efficiently, and second, it does not require a whole lot of equipment. In its simplest form, functional training can be divided into three major blocks: (1) using body weight; (2) using bands, battle ropes and pulleys (simple machines); and (3) using weights, dumb-bells, medicine balls, kettlebells, sandbags, softballs, and other such simple equipment. The beauty of functional training is that even if you are travelling for work or on a holiday, i.e., you are away from your gym, you need not feel guilty about missing your gym activity, as you can do most of the exercises without much equipment any time anywhere. There is, therefore, no long break in your regimen. In any case, however much you try, you may not be able to do all your sessions in your gym throughout the week given your hectic lifestyle and work-related pressures. Here, functional training comes as a big relief to most and this is also one major reason to shift from the traditional training available in gyms.

The most essential rule for any fitness programme is that one must avoid pain while training. When you experience pain, it is a signal that something is not right or you are overstretching your body. This is a natural feedback system to tell you to go slow—at a speed and intensity your body can handle without hurting or damaging itself. One should, therefore, follow a 'no pain' training formula all along.

Another very important aspect of exercises pertaining to functional training is that they try to mirror real-life requirements as well as support athletes and sportspersons in enhancing their throughput by providing strength, agility and flexibility in line with the activity they perform on the field.

Traditional workouts focus on exercises that are axially loaded, say top to bottom, and mostly unidirectional—for example, dead lifts and power clean. Real-life-scenario movements, especially games, are played where a player moves in several directions and needs power and flexibility in moving to almost all the directions one can think of. This is a multiple force vector scenario. Training in multidirectional force vectors is also necessary to reduce chances of injury as you prepare the body for overall stress.

Traditional strength and power training, therefore, mostly fails to bring about improvements in a person's change of direction ability. Instead, using exercises that mimic the demands of change of direction more closely, such as lateral jump training, have been shown to be effective at improving change of direction performance in sports.

A holistic training programme addressed by functional training covers the following basic movement patterns:

1. Squat
2. Push
3. Pull
4. Hinge
5. Lunge
6. Twist
7. Carry

Let us now look at each of these blocks in some detail. This will help you understand the basic philosophy underlying functional training and hence relate the exercises given later in the book to the fundamentals of the training that you will undertake. You will be able to appreciate why you are doing what you are doing.

Body weight

Functional training banks on your own weight. (It is enough to give you more than adequate exercise if used to your advantage.) Body positioning and control is at the core of body-weight training. Before loading your body with external weights and adding speed and agility to your training programme, it is important to get hold of your body and work on those functions that it is naturally designed for.

Exercises related to body weight will be given a detailed treatment in later chapters, but let us look at some basic exercises that use your body weight. There can be scores of variations in such exercises.

- *Basic push-up*: This can be done in two steps. The first is a 'plank' where you assume a stabilized push-up position and hold your body in that position for a specific time. This is good for shoulder stability and adds strength to your core. Keep your shoulder blades flat.

  After you have done this, start your workout by doing as many push-ups as you can manage to comfortably.
- *Step up*: This is good for strengthening of the legs and bringing about hip stability and extension. Here, a box of a certain height is placed in front of you and you step up on to the box with one leg, followed by the other, and then climb down with the leg lifted second, descending first, followed by the other. You could do a set with one leg and then another set with the other leg. To increase the degree of difficulty, raise the height of the box or even carry dumb-bells or a medicine ball while climbing up and down the box.
- *X-up*: This helps develop the diagonal core muscles and is great for building body strength. It also helps with combat sports like kick-boxing and mixed martial art. Lie down on the floor on your back in an X position (arms and legs opened out, the feet pointing out). Now

bring your right hand and left foot up so that the right hand touches the inside arch of the left foot. Alternate with the right arm touching the left foot and the left arm touching the right foot.

- *45-degree Calf pump*: This helps to develop strength in your ankles and build running speed.

  Stand in front of a wall. Put your hands, extended, on the wall and let your body lean at a 45-degree position resting on the hands, with both feet flat on the ground. Taking the body weight on the right foot, raise the left knee and foot up to a running position, i.e., to a chest level. Then, perform mini ankle pumps you're your left leg without allowing the heel to touch the ground. Perform this with each leg for a prescribed amount of time.

  A variation of this can be 45-degree wall run where you simulate a running motion one leg and foot at a time (while the ball of the other foot is still on the ground).

- *Vertical jump*: This is excellent for achieving hip power needed for vertical jumps and builds strength in the lower limbs. Here, you first stand straight with your legs comfortably apart. The hands could be behind your head (prisoner position), on the sides or on the hips. Squat, go as low as possible, and then explode up into a vertical jump keeping the body fully stretched while in the air. Then, land softly on both feet. Repeat as desired.

You will realize that though these exercises seem simple, they can be pretty difficult when you begin. But increasingly, as you get into a better shape, your body becomes more supple and powerful. Clearly, there are a large number of exercises that help you build strength using your body weight without using any equipment.

Bands, battle ropes and pulleys

Sports, athletics and even our day-to-day movements do not happen in single a plane. Even when you are working on the computer in your office, you often bend backwards, sideways and in several directions at the same time. When you turn around and speak to your colleague who is on another desk, you are involuntarily making a very complex movement. Now, when you have a stiff neck, imagine how difficult it is turn your head to the left or right or even to call for a glass of water.

Similarly, while playing, a player has to apply force in different directions and not necessarily in just a vertical or a horizontal plane. For instance, in cricket, a fielder who runs across to take catch a ball runs in a zigzag pattern, lunges forwards or sideways to catch the ball and at the same time curls his body, suddenly decelerating his speed to align with the falling ball and falls on the ground in the most awkward position with the ball in his hand. This is just one example of how we operate in a nonlinear fashion all the time. Movements are, so to speak, multidirectional.

In scientific terms, vector has a speed and a directional component. Hence the idea of vector as a component in physical training was appreciated and introduced. Force vector training has recently been popularized by Bret Contreras, author of several books on fitness, and it involves characterizing movement by the direction of the resistance. In theory, by using training exercises in the same force vector as the sport-specific movement, there will be a greater training transfer effect for which the training is being undertaken.

Force vector training, therefore, allows coaches to identify training exercises that are more specific to the competition movements. For example, Contreras states that since the hip thrust is performed in the anteroposterior force vector (front to back), it may have better transference on the field during sports activities that are dependent upon horizontal force production (e.g., rugby, sprinting, football).

There are six primary force vectors. They are:

- Axial—top to bottom
- Anteroposterior—front to back
- Lateromedial—outside to inside
- Posteroanterior—back to front
- Torsional—twisting and rotating
- Axial/Anteroposterior blend

For holistic training that develops strength along these force vectors, bands, ropes and pulleys are important. Once you have mastered the body weight exercises briefly explained above to control and stabilize your body, exercises based on pulleys and ropes will help you build rotational movement and deceleration.

Some of the popular equipment in this genre is illustrated below. Some basic exercises are also given to make you understand the genesis of this block.

Let us look at some of these exercises involving pulleys and bands.

- Staggered stance single-leg anterior deadlift
  a. Exercise basics
  b. Movement
  c. Benefits
- Simple deadlift
- Staggered stance incline press
- Staggered stance decline press
- Staggered stance alternating press

Battle Ropes

In a battlefield scenario, ropes sometimes become a life support system for a soldier, and several obstacles and exercise variants in military training are designed using this simple, innocent-looking rope.

Some of the most essential obstacles are:

- Burma bridge
- Parallel ropes crossing
- Vertical rope climbing
- Tarzan swing
- Rappelling against a wall or cliff assault
- Cobweb wall
- Monkey crawl on a horizontal rope

If intelligently integrated, ropes provide an excellent format for strength training in a gym as well. Most often used in a gym scenario is a long, thick rope (1–2 inch-diameter) tied to a firm object called an anchor.

These ropes may vary in length from 25 feet to 50 feet. When used in training, they are wrapped around an anchor point and each half-length is stretched out. This means, that for a 50-foot rope, the user needs to stand approximately 25 feet away from the anchor point. At each end there is usually a grip of leather or thick cloth so that it is easy to hold it with one hand each. Battle ropes can provide a high-intensity, whole-body workout that gets your muscles moving in new ways. Using battle ropes is a dynamic, ever-changing form of movement that has the added benefit of showing you whether you're doing the movements correctly. They are definitely not light in weight and require considerable effort to work out with. High-intensity interval training with battle ropes has been shown to have the potential of improving both aerobic and anaerobic parameters in just four weeks' time.

Primarily, they are regarded as a tool to train and strain the upper body. They have other benefits too, like building your abs, glutes and back muscles. They are excellent for strengthening the arms and shoulder muscles in any case. Battle ropes involve the whole body; this means that it is not only the neuromuscular system but also each individual muscle system that gets a great workout. It significantly impacts your cardio system, strengthens your grip and maximizes your power—especially in the shoulders, back and arms.

The longer and thicker the rope, the more force you'll need to use to make the waves. The slack allowed in the rope will also determine intensity. The closer you move to the anchor point, the more resistance you'll be creating.

The more movements you incorporate (such as side-to-side, up and down, or in circular motion), the more you'll work different muscles and increase your shoulder mobility and range of motion.

- *Waves:* An alternating pattern with the primary direction of force towards the anchor. This is the most often used and popular too. Although it appears simple, it can literally be a backbreaking workout. The basic variants of this movement to start with are:
  - *Double wave:* To start, stand facing the anchor with your feet shoulder-width apart. Grasp one end of the rope in each hand so that your palms face each other. Bend your knees slightly, brace your core, and move both arms up and down rapidly, creating waves in the rope.
  - *Alternating wave:* Stand facing the anchor point with your feet shoulder-width apart and knees slightly bent. Grab one end of the rope in each hand so that your palms face in. Raise one arm to shoulder level and then quickly lower your back to begin the movements raising the other arm to the shoulder level as you do so. Continue alternating the ropes as rapidly as possible without losing your form.
- *Slam:* An aggressive movement with the primary direction of force down towards the ground.
- *Whip:* A symmetrical pattern with the primary direction of force towards the anchor as if whipping an object with a thick rope.

Using the ropes in a series of linear and circular motions works as a high-intensity interval training tool (HITT). It's a tough yet effective workout, which must find place in a gym and be included in a workout schedule planned for an individual. But it is also fun as ropes are a great way to inject variety and a new kind of intensity into your exercise routine. You can work out with fitness ropes anywhere there is enough space for the ropes and an anchor. You can use them at the gym, at home, or in your backyard.

Another variation of ropes used in gyms is vertical rope climb. The individual climbs up a vertical rope using his arms and legs (squeezing the rope between both legs). As you gain more strength, this can be attempted without using your legs, with you moving up with the strength of your arms alone.

Weights, dumb-bells, medicine balls and kettlebells

After using your own body weight and thereby mastering stability, body positioning and control, and gaining all that you can in terms of force vector strength and agility by using pulleys and ropes, it is time to move on to weights.

In this section, we have dumb-bells, medicine balls and kettlebells. Again, these are neat and clean items which give you the maximum output as far as strength training by way of externally loading your body is concerned.

Earlier, fitness training was related to machine weights. The more the machines, the better it would be—this was the general feeling amongst trainers and trainees. Of late, it has been realized that machines do not give you adequate, wholesome exercise, and using them could also cause injury. In addition, if weight machines are your only source of 'resistance exercises', then you are not exercising all the muscles as you would with free weights. You are working in a fixed plane and machines do not cater for motor and rotational functions that you need while lifting weights in real life. Therefore, although you may be exercising, you will have difficulty picking up a child or loading bags and suitcases in the boot of your car.

In exercises like leg press, leg curls, and dozens of exercises on a pec deck machine, like butterfly, chest fly, building boulder shoulders or a reverse pec, you are mostly moving a secured weight up and down or in a horizontal plane all the time. These machines restrict your movement to one direction at a time.

Free weights do the exact opposite—they allow for unlimited potential movement patterns and an infinite level of resistance. They provide you a real-life experience and functional mobility and these exercises can be done throughout your life as much as you wish to.

Equipment in this genre is illustrated below. Some basic exercises are also given to make you understand the genesis of this block.

Medicine Ball

This simple-looking ball is one of the most versatile pieces of equipment for exercising your entire body. Almost 3,000 years old, it hails from a time when wrestlers and gladiators in Persia used sand-filled bladders for building strength. So, it is one of the most ancient tools for rehabilitation and building endurance. In Greece too, Hippocrates used sand-filled animal hides for injury prevention and rehabilitation. It was and still is one of the most used pieces of equipment in the armed forces.

Medicine balls are of different types and come in varied sizes:

- Softballs
- Rigid balls
- Balls with handles
- Semi-rigid throwing balls

Medicine ball basics

Both slam balls and medicine balls can be found in weights ranging from 1 kg to 20 kg (2–50 lbs). The size typically ranges from roughly the size of a handball to slightly larger than a basketball. A medicine or slam ball can be used to create a variety of exercises simply by holding the ball while performing the exercise. Both kinds of balls also work for partner exercises such as chest passes, overhead passes and rotational abdominal work where buddies twist and turn to pass the ball to each other.

While medicine balls are used as resistance and weights, slam balls are deployed for throws and passes. Actually, both can be used interchangeably. Both are weighted balls, which you can use to enhance your workout routine. The differences between the two are not many but should be considered to ensure you get the right and proper equipment for appropriate exercises.

Whether the medicine ball weight is right for you or not depends on the ball's effect on your speed of movement, precision, body control, balance or range of motion. When the medicine ball is too heavy, your motor skills, agility and stamina decline, resulting in poor form and technique that can eventually lead to injuries.

Functional fitness training involves complex movements; and so, working with medicine balls takes a bit of understanding and learning. The walking lunge with a twist engages your arms, core and legs, and requires strength, balance and flexibility. In this case, too heavy a ball and your form will break down as the stronger muscles compensate for the weaker ones. Begin with a lighter ball instead and make sure you are comfortable with this before progressing to heavier weights.

The size of your medicine ball also depends on the size of your body. For those with small hands and a small frame, a medicine ball that is 4–6 inches in diameter should be good to go. The smaller-diameter balls are also lighter and easy to grip. For those with larger hands and a larger body structure, medicine balls that are larger would go well—such as those that are 10 inches and heavier. For women, upper body strength is generally less than a man's, so you should start with a lighter ball when performing upper body exercises and gradually work your way up to the heavier balls.

We recommend starting at 40–50 per cent of your one-repetition maximum (1 RM) load. For example, if you can do biceps curl with a 15-kg weight once, this is your 1 RM. This means you should start medicine ball biceps curl with not more than 6–7.5 kg. Perform as many reps as you can comfortably without straining yourself. In general, if you are training for strength, go for the big and heavier weights, and when training for speed, go for smaller and lighter ones.

Let us look at some exercises using a medicine ball:

1. Grips

- Shoulder position
- Zercher position
- Overhead position

2. Lower body exercises

- *Zercher squat jump:* Here you adopt the Zercher standing position holding the ball in your arms and bend the legs to full squat position. Jump up explosively and land softly to regain balance. Repeat as many times as possible.
- *Overhead squat:* Stand with your legs comfortably apart lifting the ball over your head. Bend the legs and go as low as possible, then stand up slowly to complete the exercise.
- *Step jump with medicine ball:* Place one or two steps in front of you. Take the Zercher position. Bend down and take a short leap on top of the steps, stabilize and then step down (without jumping).
- *Burpee:* After adopting a frog position, you lean on the ball, push your legs backwards, keeping the spine straight and then draw the legs back together to the starting position. You then stand up and hold the ball with your hands above your head. Go back to the frog position and repeat. This is a difficult exercise that works your entire hip and back as well as the core. It is akin to the Surya Namaskar in yoga.
- *One leg deadlift:* With the medicine ball placed in front of you on the ground, lift the right leg backwards, and

taking the weight on the left foot, bend forward and grab the ball; your spine should be aligned horizontally to the ground. Now grabbing the ball, stand up slowly and return to the starting position.

3. Upper body exercises

- *Crossover push-up:* Take a push-up position with the right hand resting on the ground and the left hand on the ball. Bend the arms and perform a push- up. Move up quickly and switch position of hands and again perform a push-up. Do this repeatedly. This is a tough exercise and stretches the triceps, deltoid, pectoralis and rhomboid muscles. Do make sure to not to overstretch and spread the arms too far. (Shoulder-width is sufficient.)
- *Diamond push-up:* Put both your hands on the ball lying on the ground and move your feet back in a push-up position. Now, with the tips of your thumbs and index fingers touching each other, make a diamond. Next, bend the arms to do push down till the chest touches the ball. Now push up to straighten the arms. Repeat. This exercise helps strengthen the chest, triceps and shoulder muscles as well as the fingers, wrists and hands.
- *Bench press with medicine ball:* Lie down with your legs folded at the knees, your feet on the ground. Take the ball in your hands and bring it to your chest. Throw the ball up above your chest in the air, catch it at descent, and again throw it immediately after catching. Repeat.

- *Diagonal press:* Stand in the Zercher position with your feet apart. Bend your legs, take your arms up and push the ball diagonally to the right. Your legs support the movement and become straight as the torso moves up. Bring the ball down to chest level (starting position) and repeat in the other direction. Execute reps as required.
- *Two-arm balance press:* Stand with your feet apart and one medicine ball in one hand, palms upward. Raise both arms together slowly till your arms are straight and fully stretched out. Now bring them down slowly. Repeat.

4. Abdomen exercises

- *Arms on double ball plank:* Set up two medicine balls of equal size on the ground shoulder width apart. Acquire the plank position with arms straight and feet apart (on your toes). Exhale and keep your shoulder blades (scapulae) stabilized. Hold for a preset time. This builds your core and abdominal strength.
- *Front kneeling rotation:* Adopt a front kneeling position with the butt muscles (glutes) raised off the knees, spine straight. Hold the ball with both hands in front of you, arms straight, extending downwards. Turn the torso and arms to the left, contracting the abdominal muscles slightly. Now rotate your trunk explosively to the right, as if throwing the ball upwards, moving from low to high. Then return to the starting position, hands in front, down. Repeat on the other side. This

makes your middle body, hip muscles and abdominal muscles strong. As a variant, you can throw the ball to a partner and then catch it as he throws it back. This is a great exercise.

- *Half kneeling rotation:* Sit kneeling on your left knee, keeping your right knee up, thigh parallel to the ground. Hold the ball, contract your abdominal muscles and rotate the trunk to the left. Now from this position, move, rotating your trunk explosively to the right, as if throwing the ball upwards, moving from low to high. Come back to starting position. Do this as per preset goal. Now do this kneeling the right knee. This is a very difficult exercise which is nevertheless great for abdominal and torso strength.
- *Reverse crunch:* Lie face up (supine position) holding the ball between the knees, with your hands behind your head. Inhale and squeeze the ball between your legs, then exhale and move your knees towards the chest. Inhale and move to starting position. This is an excellent exercise for the abdomen and hip muscles.
- *Medicine ball plank position load on forearms:* Kneeling on the ground, place two balls in front and place both forearms on the two balls, one on each, palms facing inwards. Extend one leg back first, then the other, with your feet shoulder-width apart; the weight should be on your toes, your spine should be straight and the body, too, straight like a plank. You will feel the pull on the abdominal muscles and load on your hips.

Dumb-bells and kettlebells

These are used for exercising by both professionals as well as beginners. The grip, purpose and handling are different for both.

Dumb-bells come in different shapes and weights. Starting from 1 kg (2 lbs), they are available in up to 20 kg (45 lbs). The dumb-bell weight that is most suitable for you depends on your goals and your previous experience with weight training. We believe that you need to lift weights heavy enough to fatigue your muscles within a specific repetition range. Once you have completed your set you should feel that fatigue or burn in your muscles; otherwise, you need to increase the load.

You should select the weight according to the target muscle group. For weaker triceps muscles, start with 1–2 kg weights and go for 2–5 kg ones for bicep curls. Since your legs and back are much stronger, squats and other exercises for legs and torso can take up to 20 kg.

Kettlebells are available from 4 kg to 20 kg. Men usually can start with 12 kg, move up to 16 kg and go up to 20 kg. Women should start from 6 to 8 kg and go up to 12 kg. The ideal weight for your regimen is a subjective thing and also depends on your own body weight, state of fitness and your goals.

Common exercises for dumb-bells and kettlebells

You can do these exercises with either dumb-bells or kettlebells, referred to in this section as 'equipment'.

- *Single-arm swing:* Hold the equipment in the right hand with your arm parallel to the ground, palm facing downwards and feet shoulder-width apart. Now swing it down, moving the equipment between your legs like a pendulum towards the back, and then using the entire body, quickly propel the equipment up in a semi-circular path till the equipment is up to the shoulder level in front of your body. When swinging the equipment, the knees can be slightly bent. Repeat this as per your set requirement. Now do this with the other arm. This proves excellent in strengthening your ankles, knees and hips.

- *Basic squats:* With your feet shoulder-width apart, stand straight with the equipment in both hands and bring it to level of the shoulder, arms bent at the elbows, palms facing in. Keeping your core tight, equipment in place, squat as low as possible till your thighs are parallel to the ground. Gradually stand up to return to the starting position. Repeat as desired.
- *Romanian single-legged deadlift:* Hold the equipment in the right hand, palm facing inwards, arm hanging downwards, parallel to body. Balancing on the left foot with the right leg slightly bent at the knee, lift the right leg back and as you do so, bend forward so that the leg and the body are parallel to the ground. Keep looking ahead of you. Hold the position for a while and come back to the original standing position. Do this for both sides of the body as per your desired set.
- *Basic lunge:* Stand straight, feet slightly apart with the equipment in both hands, the latter pointing downwards, their palms facing inwards. Take a big step with the right foot and land in a split stance. It should be a long step so that the right knee is above

the heel/ankle, and the thigh almost parallel to ground. The left foot should stay as it is, with the toe touching the ground. Focus on the balance while raising the equipment, making it reach the side of the right foot. Once you are fully stretched, push the left foot down and use your glutes and hamstrings to step back to the starting position. Repeat as per your set and then do the same with the other leg. This strengthens the back, glutes and hamstrings. It does not strain the knees or ankles.

- *Lateral lunge:* Stand straight, feet slightly apart, arms straight down and equipment grasped in both hands, palms inwards. In this exercise, you lunge to one side at a time. Move your left foot leftwards so that your foot lands at a distance double your shoulder width; weights to the left, bending at the waist, bring both weights down to each side of the left foot, torso parallel to the ground. Now from this position, push the left foot and butt muscles and move back to start position. Repeat for the same side first and then do this with the other foot and repeat.

Some specific exercises using kettlebells

A kettlebell is a cast-iron or cast-steel weight that looks like a cannonball, or a throw ball with a handle, which makes it easier to execute swinging movements. Kettlebells date back to the seventeenth century and do find mention in some Russian literature. These equipment were earlier used as weights to weigh products sold by merchants in Asia and the Far East, including Russia. Russians measured weights in poods, where 1 pood is equivalent to 16.38 kg. These were later used for exercise in Europe and then they reached America from where they became a popular exercising tool across the fitness industry.

Let as look at a few specific exercises using this equipment:

- *Box squat:* Stand upright holding a kettlebell with both hands in front of a step about 15 inches high. With your arms bent at the elbows, pull the kettlebell close to the chest, almost touching your chin. Then, move your pelvis backwards, bend your legs and sit on the step. After a pause, rise back to the original position. Repeat. This kind of a squat helps build hip muscles, and strengthens arms, wrists and legs.
- *Walking lunge with overhead weight:* First, with your feet shoulder-width apart, you stand holding one kettlebell above your head. Then, you take a step forward with the left leg, lowering the right knee to a kneeling position, the latter touching the ground. Now, rise, then do the same with the right leg forward and lowering your left knee to the kneeling position. Keep moving forward in this sequence. This is a wholesome exercise that involves the entire hip extensor chain muscles and is great for building strength in arms, legs, especially wrists and the quadriceps chain. It also trains your abdominal muscles and trapezius muscles.
- *Windmill or triangle action:* Stand with feet apart shoulder-width holding a kettlebell in the right hand, and move the right arm up straight into the air, above your head. The other kettlebell is on the ground in front of the left foot. Move the left foot slightly to the left diagonally. Bend from your waist down to the left,

looking at the kettlebell in the right hand up above your head. Keep your legs as straight as possible, and reach out to the other kettlebell on the ground near the left foot. Now grasp the handle of the kettlebell on the ground in front of your left foot and straighten your body slowly, right arm still above the head and straight up, left arm pointing straight down.

Other interesting equipment

Sandbag and softball are two very important items used effectively in functional training. Let us look at both of these.

Sandbag

Sandbags were used by the army because soldiers had to carry a lot of weight in backpacks and get used to carrying them during long marches. Since sandbags were used for building bunkers and trenches as well, they were easily available to be used as physical training tools.

For gyms, these are bags made like a duffel bag with strong synthetic material filled with sand or something similar. Also referred to as power bags, these typically have two handles and a single grip on the outside for someone to hold it and use for different exercises. They usually weigh from 3 kg to 20 kg apiece.

K Bags have six handles and three different grips.

The basic grips are:

- *Zercher grip:* Using the middle grip, hold it close to the chest to the shoulder level, arms spread shoulder-width, with your spine straight.

- *On the shoulder grip:* The arm encircles the bag kept on one of the shoulders, close to the ear.
- *Overhead position:* Push the bag above the head holding it firmly with both hands. The arms are to be kept straight, and the head slightly forward. This helps strengthen the spine and the back.

Some basic exercises you can try with the bag:

- *Deadlift at the shoulder:* With the bag between your legs, sit down in a squat position, holding the bag with the middle grip. Move the bag to the left shoulder explosively, stabilizing it with the left arm as an overgrip. Repeat for the other side. This is a total body functional exercise.
- *Kneeling jump and snatch:* Kneel with your toes touching the ground, your pelvis raised, spine straight, and the bag in front. Jump to your feet, remaining in a squat position, with your arms in front, the palms facing inwards. Hold the bag through the middle grip and thrust it up over your head, arms straight in vertical position, your spine straight. Bring the bag to the Zercher position. This is a difficult exercise but a very powerful total body exercise.
- *Zercher lunge with rotation:* Using the Zercher grip, stand with your legs apart at shoulder width. the first, with your left foot, take a step forward. Then lower your body to let the right knee touch the ground, the right leg pushed back, while your left is ahead and folded. Now rotate the torso towards your left And then come back to the straight position. Now get up

and take a step forward with the right leg, bag in the centre. Lower your body into a lunge with the left knee almost touching the ground, rotate the torso to the right and return to the starting position. Repeat as desired. This is a very tough exercise and in this, functional action takes its best form. It activates the abdominal muscles and strengthens the upper as well as the lower body, especially the torso.

- *Sandbag power plyo push-up:* First, get into a push-up position with your hands on the bag, holding it through the middle grip, your arms extended shoulder-width apart. The feet should be comfortably apart, the body resting straight on the toes for balance. Now bend your arms like in a push-up dip until your chest rests on the sandbag. Then straighten the arms explosively and raise your torso upwards with the bag moving upwards from the ground. Then land and stabilize before you do the next round. This is a tough exercise that focuses on the upper part of the body, torso and gut muscles. But it counts for good training for all combat sports and martial arts.
- *Potato sandbag push-up:* Start with the push-up position, with the sandbag on the ground between your hands. Dip, till your chest touches the top of the bag. Take the arms explosively upwards in the air. Now land both hands simultaneously on top of the bag. Again, extend your arms explosively in the air, returning to the starting position with the hands on the ground. Repeat the desired number of times. This is tougher than a regular push-up and great for back muscles, torso and entire upper body.

Softball or stability ball

Stability balls were initially used to provide an unstable training surface. As functional training evolved, trainers and researchers found other effective ways to use these. Now these equipment are also used to provide a rolling surface to enable natural movement and instability. In addition, these support dynamic positions in a stationary environment. They help create exercises and movements to build cardio endurance, balance, and overall strength as well as aid in stretching muscles. These balls are usually available in different sizes: 55 cm, 65 cm and 75 cm diameter.

Let us look at a few exercises using this equipment:

- *Hamstring curl:* Lie on your back on the ground with your arms straight, palms on the ground, and fingers pointing towards the feet, and the ball near your feet. Now put your feet up and let your heels touch the ball. Then, pull your legs back, lifting the hips and the lower back, and pull the ball back towards your head. Hold for a while and then move the legs towards the feet. It is like a roller action, moving front and back. It helps build and stretch the back.
- *Balance push-up:* Lie on your stomach on the ball, with your hands and feet touching the ground, and move forward walking on your hands till your shins touch the ball. Now keeping your arms straight in a push-up position, do a dip and repeat as many dips as you can. This exercise is great for the arms, biceps and building a strong back.

- *Back stretch:* Start with the stomach and hips on the ball, legs extended straight behind (toes resting on the ground). Hold on to the ball with the hands for balance. If this position is difficult to maintain, try placing the feet against a wall. Raise the chest high (like a yoga 'cobra'), bringing the hands to the back of the head. Hold for a beat or two, then return to a relaxed position. Repeat as many times as you are comfortable.

Thus far, we have provided a detailed coverage of most types of exercises that are deployed for functional fitness under each of these blocks. And this should give you an idea of the basics of functional training so that you are clear about what functional training entails in totality.

Gyms are like '*fitness Satsang*'

We had mentioned in the beginning of the chapter that one major advantage of functional fitness is that you do not require big complex machines to do it. The absence of complex equipment also allows you to engage in these exercises when you are away from your gym on a holiday or work-related travel.

Yet we would like to emphasize that gyms provide you a conducive environment where *you feel like exercising*. It provides you some kind of binding force, one that pushes you to follow a routine. It ensures that you allocate some time in a day for fitness. Think about it: Why do so many people give up on fitness when they try to make a routine to work out at home but are unable to sustain this activity? They give up because they have no company to motivate them. If you look at it, many people go for a morning walk in a small group, because each person of the group motivates the other to wake up in the morning and come together for a walk. They not only walk but also chat a little and become good friends and walking partners. Similarly, in golf, you cannot play alone on the course; it is so boring. That is why people make a four ball and push each other as if in a mini competition.

Sustenance and regularity is the key to fitness and this can be provided only by a gym setting. There you find a group of people who are struggling with similar problems and have matching goals and aspirations. Remember, in a herd of say fifty horses who are running, the weak ones also learn to run and are motivated to run as the good ones provide a 'mental push' to the weaker ones. Similarly, you get a lot of encouragement when you see thirty people around you working out. That sweat and grinding, all that heaving and puffing, provide you a kick that can build up that adrenaline that one desperately needs to keep going.

Take another example. You can pray at home. Then why do people go to the temple, church, or gurdwara or mosque? This is to bind you to a ritual where everyone prays collectively. Many people go to listen to talks by spiritual gurus in a setting where there are thousands of people who equally want to listen to sermons about good values and ideas of great men and women. These are called 'satsang'—'sat' (pronounced as in sub) means good, and 'sang' (pronounced as the English word 'sung') means company. It is a collective where everyone is spiritually inclined and thinks in a positive way.

Gyms could be considered to be equivalent to such satsangs. They are like temples of fitness that provide you not only with a facility where you can exercise but also a place where you can socialize and make friends with those who are 'fitness-minded'.

So go for it!

BODY WEIGHT EXERCISES

I. Lower Body

1. **Calf raises**

    - Stand with the balls of your feet on the edge of the step/block and let your heels drop down as far as possible.
    - Slowly raise your heels up as high as possible.
    - Pause, and then slowly lower your heels back to the starting position.
    - Do not rest at the bottom, and immediately start the next rep.
    - Repeat for desired number of repetitions (reps).

2. **Jump squats**
   - Stand with your feet shoulder-width apart.
   - Start by doing a regular squat, then engage your core and jump up explosively.
   - When you land back on your feet, lower your body back into the squat position to complete one rep. Land as quietly as possible.
   - Repeat for desired number of reps.

3. **Lunges and rotations**

- Stand tall with your feet hip-width apart.
- Step forward with one foot and slowly lower your body into a lunge. Your front knee should be bent to at least 90 degrees and your rear knee should be a few inches off the floor.
- As you lunge, rotate your upper body towards your lead leg. Make sure you are rotating from your upper back—not your lower back.
- Pause, and return to the starting position.

4. **Glute bridges**

- Lie face up on the floor, with your knees bent and feet flat on the ground. Keep your arms at your side, your palms down on the floor.
- Lift your hips off the ground until your knees, hips and shoulders form a straight line. Squeeze those glutes hard and keep your abs drawn in so you don't overextend your back during the exercise.
- Hold your bridged position for a couple of seconds before easing back down.

II. Upper Body

5. **Back extensions**
    - Lie on your stomach, face down, arms straight out in front of you, palms down, and legs straight out behind you.
    - Pull your abs in, as if you are trying to create a small space between your stomach and the floor.
    - Lift your left arm and right leg about one inch off the floor, and stretch out as much as you can.
    - Hold this position for five slow counts and then lower your arm and leg back down.
    - Repeat the same move with your right arm and left leg.
    - Continue alternating sides until you complete the set.

6. **Close grip push-up**
    - Lie on the floor face down and place your hands closer than shoulder width for a close hand position. Make sure that you are holding your torso up at arms' length.
    - Lower yourself until your chest almost touches the floor as you inhale.
    - Using your triceps and some of your pectoral muscles, press your upper body back up to the starting position and squeeze your chest. Breathe out as you perform this step.
    - After a second pause at the contracted position, repeat the movement for the prescribed number of repetitions.

7. **Pull-ups**

- Grasp a pull-up bar in a grip slightly wider than shoulder width, with your palms facing away from you.
- Hang freely from the bar, arms stretched out above you.
- Bend at the knees if there is not enough clearance below you.
- Pull your body up so that your neck reaches the level of the bar.
- Slowly descend back to the starting position.
- Repeat for the desired number of repetitions.

8. Chin ups

- Grasp a pull-up bar with a shoulder width under hand (supinated) grip.
- Hang freely from the bar, arms fully extended.
- Pull body upwards until your neck is level with the bar.
- Slowly descend back to the starting position.
- Repeat for the desired number of reps.

III. Full Body

9. **Military burpee**
    - Start by standing tall with your feet about shoulder-width apart. Then bend your knees and squat while bringing your hands to the ground.
    - With control, thrust your feet back into a plank position. Don't let your hips drop.
    - Complete a push-up with proper form, then pull your feet forward to meet your hands, and immediately jump straight up off the ground.

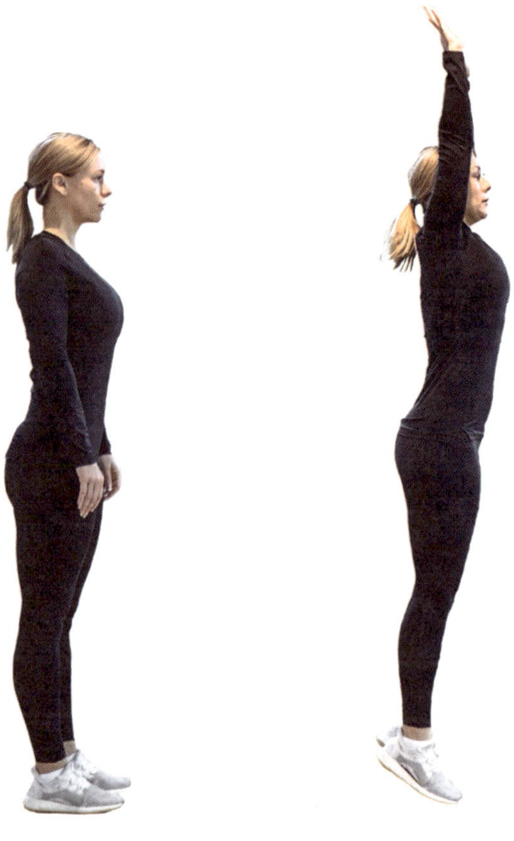

- Land softly into the squat position, and repeat. Hands down, thrust back, push up, jump forward, jump up.
- Find a continuous rhythm, and remember to breathe.

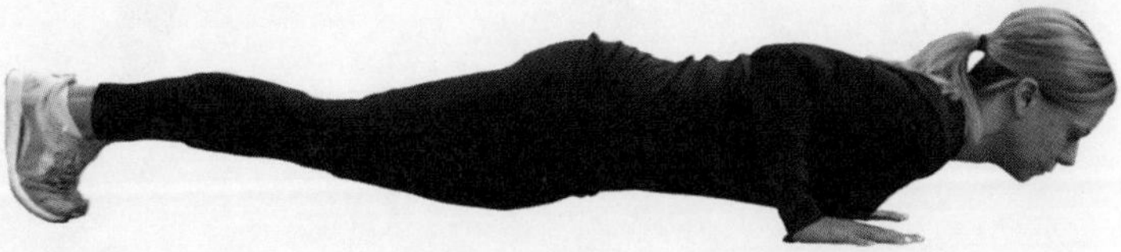

10. Inchworm

- Stand with your feet close together. Keeping your legs straight, stretch down and put your hands on the floor directly in front of you. This will be your starting position.
- Begin by walking your hands forward slowly, alternating your left and your right. As you do so, bend only at the hip, keeping your legs straight.
- Keep going until your body is parallel to the ground in a push-up position.
- Now, keep your hands in place and slowly take short steps with your feet, moving only a few inches at a time.
- Continue walking until your feet are by your hands, keeping your legs straight as you do so.

11. Mountain climber

- Start with your body in a straight line with your hands slightly wider than shoulder- width apart, and keep your balls and feet touching the floor.
- Bring one knee to the centre of your stomach and quickly alternate.
- Continue alternating till set is complete.

12. **Tuck jump**

- As your starting position, stand with your feet hip-width apart.
- Place your hands on the floor and kick your legs back, so that you end up with your stomach and thighs on the floor. Your elbows should be bent. From this position, press up like you're doing a push-up, extending your arms and bringing your hips off the ground.
- Now, jump so your feet reach under your hips in a squat position, then immediately explode upwards, driving your knees towards your chest.

- Jump as high as you can, raising your knees up, and then ensure a good landing by extending your legs and absorbing the impact by bending your knees.
- Repeat for the recommended number of reps.

IV Core

13. Plank

- Get in the push-up position. Only put your forearms on the ground instead of your hands. Your elbows should line up directly underneath your shoulders. Your toes should be on the ground.
- Squeeze your glutes and tighten your abdomen.

- Keep a neutral neck and spine.
- Create a straight, strong line from head to toes—a plank, if you will.
- Hold that position.

14. Side plank

- Lie on one side with your legs stacked and fully extended.
- Using your lower elbow and forearm, prop your body up, making sure you keep your abs tight the entire time. Your body should form a straight line from your shoulders up to your ankles.

15. Heel touchers

- Lie on the floor with the knees bent and the feet on the floor around 18 to 24 inches apart. Your arms should be by your side, extended, fingers pointing towards the feet. This will be your starting position.
- Crunch over your torso forward and up about 3 to 4 inches to the right and touch your right heel as you hold the contraction for a second. Exhale while performing this movement.
- Now go back slowly to the starting position while you inhale.
- Now crunch over your torso forward and up around 3 to 4 inches to the left side and touch your left heel as you hold the contraction for a second. Exhale while performing this movement and then return to the starting position as you inhale. Now that both heels have been touched, that is considered one repetition.
- Continue alternating sides in this manner until the prescribed number of repetitions is complete.

16. Dead bug

- Lie on your back with your arms relaxed by your side.
- Bend your hips and life your knees at a 90-degree angle.

- Tighten your abs and press your lower back onto the floor.
- Take a deep breath.
- As you exhale, slowly extend your left leg towards the floor. Keep your abs tight and don't let your lower back arch.
- Slowly return your leg to the starting position.
- Repeat with your opposite leg. Continue alternating for desired number of reps.

V. Abdomen

17. Crunches

- Lie on your back with your knees bent and feet flat on the floor, hip-width apart.
- Place your hands behind your head so your thumbs are behind your ears.
- Don't lace your fingers together.
- Hold your elbows out to the sides but rounded slightly in.
- Tilt your chin forward slightly, leaving a few inches of space between your chin and your chest.
- Gently pull your abdomen inwards.
- Curl up and forward so that your head, neck and shoulder blades lift off the floor.

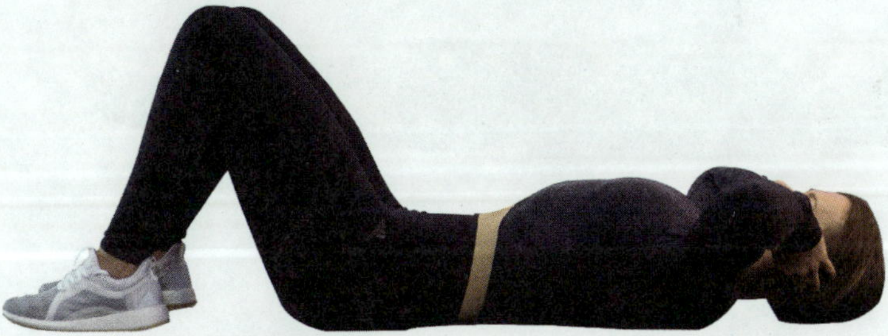

18. Leg raises

- Lie supine on a bench or a mat. Place your hands under lower back on each side to support the pelvis.
- Keeping the knees straight, raise your legs by flexing the hips until they are completely flexed. Return legs to starting position until hips and knees are extended. Repeat.

19. Flutter kicks

- Lie on your back on a gym mat with your legs extended and your arms alongside your hips, palms down.
- Lift your legs 4–6 inches off the floor. Press your low back into the mat.
- Keep your legs straight as you rhythmically raise one leg higher, then switch. Move in a fluttering, up and down motion.
- Repeat for desired number of reps.

20. Criss-crosses

- Lie flat on your back with knees bent.
- Cross your right leg on top of your left knee and support your head with the left hand.
- Crunch and bring your left elbow towards the right knee.
- Repeat for desired number of reps and switch sides.

Ropes, Pulleys and Bands

I. Lower Body

Ropes

1. **Squats with battle rope waves**
   - Holding a battle rope in each hand, bend at the knees and drive the hips back while you maintain a tight core.
   - From this squat position, bring the left rope up as you move the right rope down.
   - Immediately, bring the right rope up and move the left rope down.
   - Keep repeating this alternating motion while remaining in the squat position.

2. **Alternating lunges with battle rope waves**

- Hold a rope in each hand in a handshake grip.
- Step back into a reverse lunge while completing a battle rope wave.
- Come back to a neutral standing position but do not stop alternating waves with the battle rope.
- Switch legs and repeat the movement for desired number of reps.

3. **Lateral lunges with battle rope waves**

- Stand in a wide stance with the battle rope held in a handshake grip.
- Make simultaneous waves with the battle rope as you shift the weight to one side and perform a lateral lunge.

- Return to neutral position while continuously making battle rope waves.
- Shift weight to the other side and perform lateral lunge.
- Repeat for desired number of rep.

4. **Plyo jumps with battle rope waves**
   - Stand with feet hip width apart and battle rope held in handshake position.
   - With the battle rope held firmly in both hands, go down in a squat and jump as high as possible.
   - On landing, make simultaneous battle rope waves for 5 counts and perform a plyo jump again.
   - Repeat for desired repetitions.
   - Note: Any exercise that's going to use battle ropes will inevitably involve the upper body and core, making it a full-body workout.

Pulleys

5. **Pulley ankle dorsiflexion**

    - Attach an ankle strap to the cable pulley.
    - Wrap the strap around your ankle and elevate your foot on a bench.
    - Plantar flex your ankle to keep it relaxed, this is your starting position.
    - Dorsiflex your ankle to generate tension in the forefoot, this is the end position.
    - Repeat for desired number of reps.

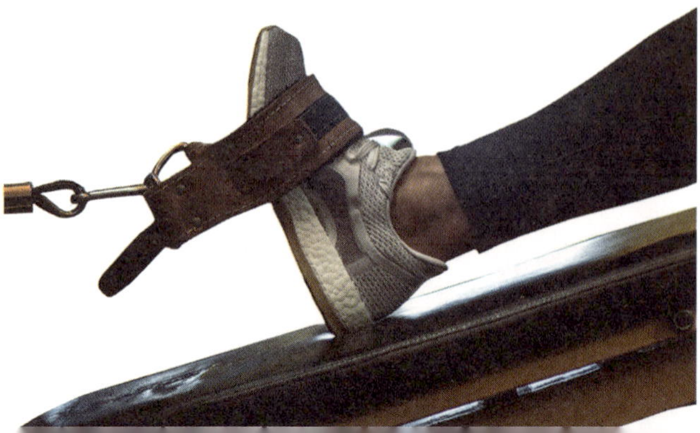

6. Hamstring curls

- Adjust the machine lever to fit your height and sit on the machine with your back against the back support pad.
- Place the back of the lower leg on top of the padded lever (just a few inches under the calves) and secure the lap pad against your thighs, just above the knees. Then grasp the side handles on the machine as you point your toes straight (or you can also use any of the other two stances) and ensure that the legs are fully straight right in front of you. This will be your starting position.
- As you exhale, pull the machine lever as far as possible to the back of your thighs by flexing at the knees. Keep your torso stationary at all times. Hold the contracted position for a second.
- Slowly return to the starting position as you breathe in.
- Repeat for the recommended number of reps.

7. **Hip adduction**

   - Stand in front of a low pulley facing forward with one leg next to the pulley and the other one away.
   - Attach the ankle cuff to the cable and to the ankle of the leg that is next to the pulley.
   - Now step out and away from the stack with a wide stance and grasp the bar of the pulley system.
   - Stand on the foot that does not have the ankle cuff and allow the leg with the cuff to be pulled towards the low pulley. This will be your starting position.
   - Now perform the movement by moving the leg with the ankle cuff in front of the far leg by using

the inner thighs to adduct the hip. Breathe out during this portion of the movement.

- Slowly return to the starting position as you breathe in.
- Repeat for the recommended number of reps and then repeat the same movement with the opposite leg.

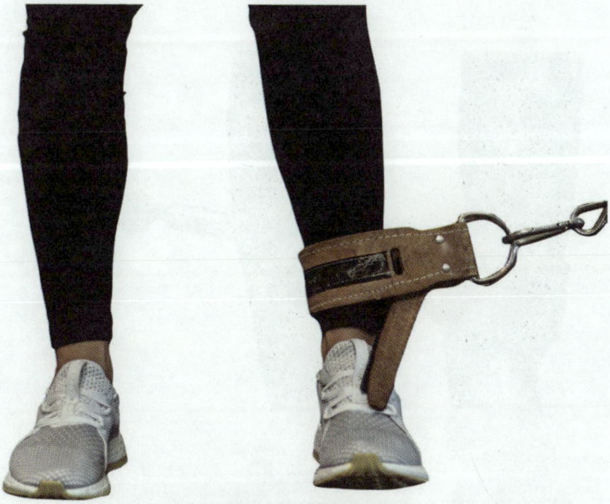

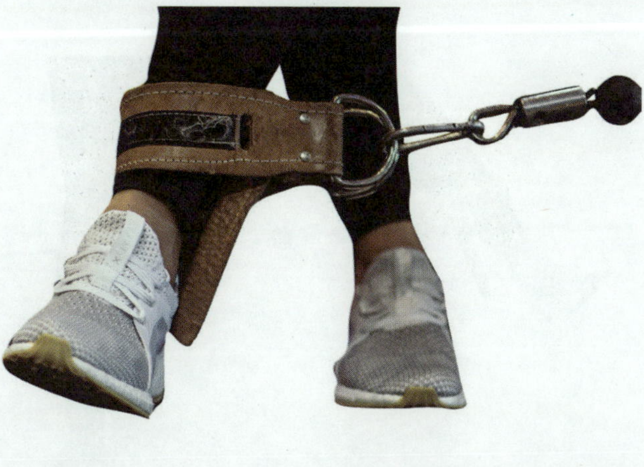

8. **Hip abduction**

    - Stand in front of low pulley facing to one side. Attach cable cuff to far ankle. Step out away from the stack and grasp the ballet bar. Stand on the near foot and allow far leg to cross in front.
    - Move leg to the opposite side of low pulley by abduction hip. Return and repeat. Turn around and continue with the opposite leg.

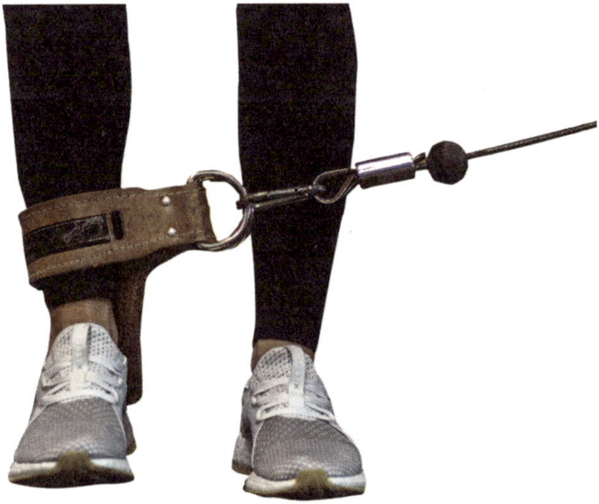

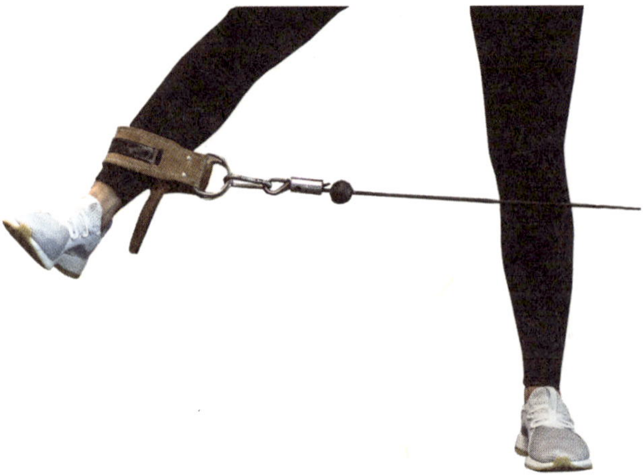

Bands

9. In and out squats

- Place a resistance band slightly above the knee in such a way that there is slight tension in the glutes when standing with feet hip width apart.
- Stand with feet together, placing your hands on the front of your thighs.
- Bend your legs, jump up and separate your feet in mid-air.
- Land with feet apart wider than hip-width, lowering in a squat. Jump out of the squat and land in the starting position.
- Repeat for desired number of reps.

10. Crab walks

- Place a resistance band appropriately tensed slightly above the knee.
- Stand with feet hip-width apart and knees rotated outwards.
- Lower yourself into a squat; this is your starting position.
- Holding yourself in the starting position take eight to ten steps towards one side.
- Repeat by taking steps towards the other side.

11. Ankle plantarflexion

- Sit on the floor with your right leg extended. Wrap one end of a resistance band around the ball of your right foot and hold the other end in your hands. Keep toes flexed.
- Slowly press your foot forward pointing it as you maintain the band's resistance, then return to the starting position.
- Repeat with your other foot.

12. Unilateral hip abduction

- Lie down on one side of the body with the knees bent at approximately 45 degrees and both feet touching each other.
- Tie an appropriately tensed resistance band above the knee.
- Raise the upper knee up without lifting the foot.
- Repeat for desired number of reps and repeat on the other side.

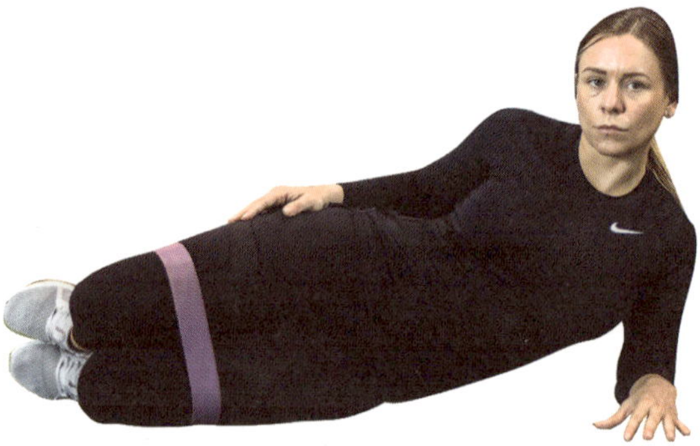

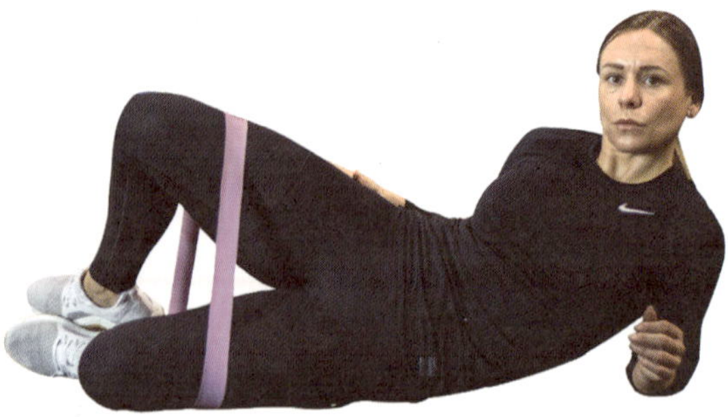

II. Upper body

Ropes

1. **Kneeling alternate battle rope waves**
    - Hold the battle ropes in a handshake grip and kneel down on one knee, keeping the other foot planted firmly on the floor.
    - From this position, bring the left rope up while you bring the right rope down.
    - Now bring the right rope up while bringing the left rope down.
    - Keep alternating this motion for the desired amount of time.

2. **Battle rope smashes**
    - Hold the battle rope in a handshake grip and stand with your feet hip-width apart.
    - Lower yourself into a squat position while keeping the core braced as straight as possible.
    - Lift both hands simultaneously and smash the battle ropes down to the ground.
    - Repeat for the desired number of reps.

3. **In 'n' out battle rope waves**
    - Hold the battle rope in a handshake grip and stand with your feet hip-width apart.

- Lower yourself in a squat position while keeping the core braced and back as upright as possible.
- Move the battle ropes in an in-and-out motion, forming waves.
- Repeat for desired number of reps.

4. **Seated rope pulls**
   - Knot one end of a battle rope to the front of a sled or to a kettlebell.
   - Stretch the rope across the floor and sit at the unweighted end.
   - Straddle the rope, knees soft, glutes and abs engaged, back hinged slightly, chest up, and heels anchored into the floor.

- Pull the rope extending your hand over another until the weight reaches your feet.
- Reset at the far end of the room.

Pulleys

5. **Triceps pushdown**
   - Attach a straight or angled bar to a high pulley and grab it in an overhand grip, your hands shoulder-width apart.

- Standing upright with the torso straight and a very slight inclination forward, bring the upper arms close to your body and perpendicular to the floor.
- Using the triceps, bring the bar down until it touches the front of your thighs and the arms are fully extended perpendicular to the floor. The upper arms should always remain stationary next to your torso and only the forearms should move.
- After a second hold at the contracted position, bring the bar slowly up to the starting point.
- Repeat it for the recommended number of reps.

6. **Lat pulldown**

    - Sit at a lat pulldown station and grab the bar with an overhand grip that is just beyond shoulder width.
    - Your arms should be completely straight and your torso upright.
    - Pull your shoulder blades down and back, and bring the bar to the level of your chest. Pause, and then slowly return to the starting position.
    - Repeat it for desired number of reps.

7. **Face pulls**

- Stand in front of a medium-height rotating pulley and grab each side of the rope attachment. Step back and away from the machine until your arms are fully extended in front of you.
- Your feet should be slightly wider than shoulder-width apart and there should be a soft bend in your knees.
- Brace core and drive the elbows past your back, while pulling the rope handles slightly outside of your ears. Hold and contract shoulder blades together.
- Repeat for desired number of reps.

8. **Pronated bicep curl**

    - Grasp the bar in an overhand grip shoulder-width.
    - Stand erect with upper arms and elbows down by your sides, stationary.
    - Flex at the elbows to curl the weight upwards by contracting the biceps. Upper arms and elbows should remain fixed to your sides.
    - After peak contraction, slowly reverse the movement back to the starting position.
    - Repeat for the desired number of reps.

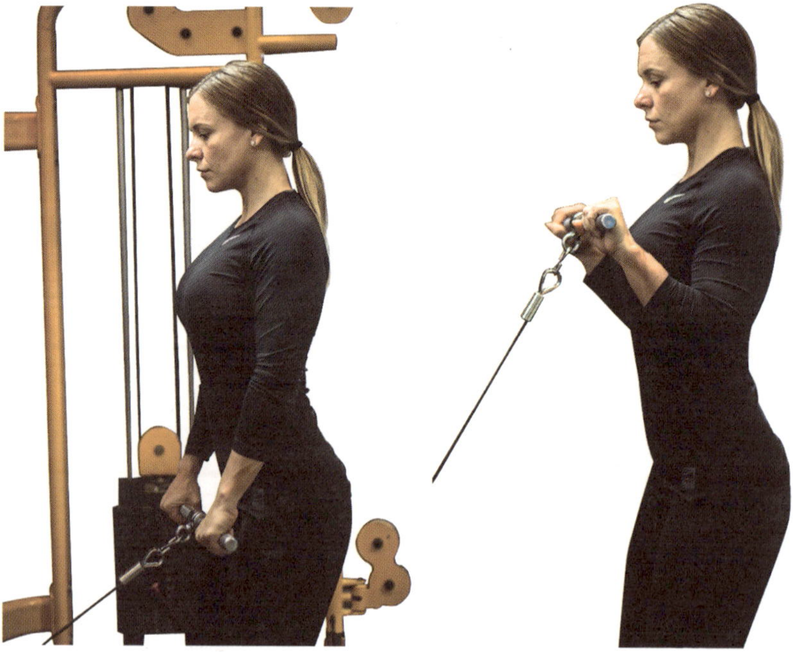

Bands

9. **Lateral raises**
    - Assume a staggered stance position. Stand on the centre of the band with the band under the front part of your feet.
    - Grasp the band on both ends and lift your arms outwards, keeping your elbows straight and thumbs up. Stop at shoulder level.
    - Hold and slowly return. Keep your shoulder blades down; avoid shrugging your shoulders. Keep your back straight.
    - Repeat for desired number of reps.

10. Front raises

- Grab a resistance band, loop it under your feet, and hold it in each hand, with your arms at your sides.
- Raise your arms straight in front of you until they are parallel to the floor and perpendicular to your torso.
- Your hands should be at the shoulder level and the thumb side of your hands should be facing up. Pause, and then slowly lower back to the starting position.
- Repeat for desired number of reps.

11. Bicep curl

- Stand with both your feet on the resistance band holding the handles long next to your sides with the palms facing forward.
- Slowly curl your hands up to your shoulders, squeezing the biceps and keeping the elbows next to your sides.
- Slowly release your arms back down to the starting position.

12. **Overhead triceps extension**

- Stand with one foot slightly in front of the other and place the centre of the band under the back foot.
- Bring handles together straight up above the top of your head.
- Slowly lower the handles behind the back of your head until the elbows are bent to 90 degrees, keeping the elbows close to the side of your head.
- Press hands back up overhead slowly.

III. Full body

Ropes

1. **Burpee to battle rope smash**
   - Hold the battle ropes in a handshake grip.
   - Perform a battle rope smash and follow it up with a burpee while holding the battle rope firmly in both hands.

- Repeat for desired number of reps.

2. **Battle rope jumping jack**
    - Hold the battle rope in both the hands using an overhand grip.
    - Stand with your feet together and hands besides the legs.
    - Jump up while pushing the feet out and lifting the battle ropes to the side till your hands are parallel to the floor.

- Jump up and feet to the starting position. This is one repetition.
- Repeat for desired number of reps.

3. **Carioca ropes**
    - Grab one battle rope in both hands and stand with your feet hip-width apart.
    - Start performing battle rope waves while simultaneously moving laterally crossing one foot over the other.
    - Take 3 steps in one direction and 3 steps in the other.
    - Repeat for desired number of reps.

Pulleys

4. **Lunge into single handed row**
   - Set the cable pulley in line with your abdomen.
   - Grab the handle in one hand with a neutral grip and take 4 steps away from the cable machine.
   - Set your feet in a split stance, such that you are able to balance yourself comfortably; keep the hand holding the handle extended and the other hand rested on your hip. This is your starting position.
   - Bend the leg that's in front to 90 degrees, in a kneeling position, hold for one second and rise. Pull the handle towards the abdomen while keeping the elbow tucked in. This is your final position.
   - Repeat for desired number of reps.

5. **Squat into bicep curl**

    - Stand with feet shoulder width apart and grab a cable bar in both hands with an underhand grip.
    - Bend your knees, push your hip back and flex your elbows squeezing your biceps.
    - Press your heel to the floor and return to the initial position.
    - Repeat for desired number of reps.

6. **Squat position row**

    - Stand with your feet shoulder-width apart, hold the two handles on the cable in a neutral grip, your hands extended. This is your starting position.

- Lower yourself into a squat and pull the cable towards your abdomen while keeping the elbows tucked in. This is your final position.
- Repeat for desired number of reps.

7. **Lunge into overhead extension using rope**
    - Set the cable pulley in the middle position and attach the rope attachment.
    - Stand with one leg in front of the other, and back facing the cable attachment. Grab the rope attachment above your head.
    - With your right leg lunge forwards keeping your back neutral and making sure both legs are at a 90 degree angle with your head facing forwards.

- Return to the original position and perform an overhead extension while keeping the elbows parallel to each other. This is one repetition.
- Repeat for desired number of reps. Once completed, change legs.

Bands

8. **Lunge with lateral shoulder raise**
    - Stand in a split stance and plant a Thera band firmly under the ball of the front foot.
    - Grab the other end of the band with appropriate tension.
    - Lower yourself into a lunge while simultaneously raising your arm laterally.
    - Return to start position and repeat the required number of reps.
    - Switch sides and repeat.

9. Squat with rotations

- Stand with your feet shoulder-width apart with resistance band tied adjacent to you around a support with your arms held in front. This is your starting position.
- Lower down into a squat until the buttocks are parallel to the floor.
- Rotate your hips 90 degrees to the left keeping the resistance band held out in front.
- Once you have completed the movement 10 times return to your starting position. Change sides and repeat the exercise by twisting 90 degrees to the right completing 10 repetitions.
- Repeat movement for desired number of sets.

10. Lunge into chest flies

- Stand in a split stance with two dumb-bells held wider than chest-width apart in a neutral grip.
- Perform a forward lunge while simultaneously bringing the dumb-bells closer to each other. Hands should be locked out at the final position.
- Return to original position.
- Repeat for desired number of reps.

IV. Core

Ropes

11. Plank position battle rope waves

- Set up in a high plank position with your palms under your shoulders, your legs fully extended, and your body forming a straight line from your head to your heels.
- Shift your weight slightly to the left side and grab the right end of the rope with your right hand.
- Maintaining a tight, strong plank, begin whipping your right arm upwards then downwards, creating a wave through the right half of the rope.
- Switch sides and repeat.

12. **Battle rope claps**

- Stand with your feet hip-width apart and hold the battle ropes in a neutral grip
- Move the hands in and out like you would when clapping.
- Repeat for desired number of reps.

Pulleys

13. **High pulley woodchoppers**

- Connect a standard handle to a tower, and move the cable to the highest pulley position.
- With your side to the cable, grab the handle

with one hand and step away from the tower. Your outstretched arm should be aligned to the cable.

- With your feet positioned shoulder-width apart, reach upwards with your other hand and grab the handle with both hands. Your arms should still be fully extended.
- In one motion, pull the handle down and across your body to your front knee while rotating your torso.

- Keep your back and arms straight and core tight while you pivot your back foot and bend your knees to get a full range of motion.
- Maintain your stance and arms straight. Return to the neutral position in a slow and controlled manner.

- Then, reposition and repeat the same series of movements on the opposite side.

14. Low pulley woodchoppers

- Assume an athletic position with your feet just wider than shoulder-width apart and attach a rope to a cable stack at the lowest position possible.
- Position the inside leg in hip extension and set up with both hands grasping the ends of the rope.

- Pull the rope to the level of the chest and then press diagonally overhead.
- Return to the starting position, repeat for the desired number of reps, and then switch sides.

15. **Mid pulley woodchoppers**

- Assume an athletic position with your feet wider than shoulder-width apart and attach a rope to a cable stack in the middle position.
- Position the inside leg in hip extension and set up with both hands grasping the ends of the rope.
- Pull the rope and rotate the trunk while keeping the hands fully extended.
- Upon reaching full rotation, return to the starting position.
- Repeat for desired number of reps.

16. Stiff arm pulldown

- Stand at an adjustable cable machine and grab the lat pulldown bar in an overhand grip that's about shoulder-width apart.
- Keep your knees slightly bent and feet shoulder-width apart.
- Exhale and pull the bar down to your thighs. Your arms should remain straight, elbows locked. Pause, and then return to the starting position.
- Repeat for desired number of reps.

Bands

17. Knee pull

- Start on the floor in push-up position with the centre of the band wrapped around the sole of your right foot, holding one end of the band in each hand, your palms flat.
- Keep the right knee flexed and close to the chest while the left knee remains extended.
- Push the right knee back without rounding the back and return to the starting position.
- Repeat for desired number of reps and switch sides.

18. Tubing half-teaser

- Lie face up on the floor with the right knee bent, foot flat, and left leg extended towards the ceiling. Fold the tube in half, then loop it around the left arch and grasp the ends together with both hands.
- Roll your torso off the floor slowly to sit up—try to use your abs, rather than pulling with your arms, by drawing the navel into the spine.
- Hold for 1 to 3 counts, then engage your abs to roll slowly back down to start.

19. Resistance band side plank

- Stand with feet hip-width apart on the centre of the tube, cross it once or twice in front of you, then grasp a handle in each hand, arms by the sides.
- Crouch down and walk hands forward to get in full push-up position.

- Shift the body weight onto the left hand and rotate the extended right arm to reach for the ceiling while keeping your shoulders down.
- Hold for 1 to 3 counts, and then return to full push-up.

V. Abdomen

Ropes

20. **Battle rope crunches**

- Sit on the floor with your legs out straight in front of you and spread slightly apart.
- Grab the battle ropes together in your hands and, while making waves with the ropes, slowly lower your torso back so that you almost touch the ground.

- Pull your torso back up.

21. Battle rope Russian twists

- Sit on the ground with your legs straight and slightly bent in front of you.
- While gripping the rope with both hands, lean back slightly. Then, slam them down on either side of your body while twisting your torso.

- Repeat for desired duration.

22. Boat position smashes

- Sit on the floor with your legs slightly bent in front of you.
- Then, lift your legs and lean your torso back at a 45-degree angle.
- Grip a rope in each hand and make alternating waves.
- Repeat for desired duration.

23. Boat position circular smashes

- Sit on the floor with your legs slightly bent in front of you.
- Then, lift your legs and lean your torso back at a 45-degree angle.
- Grip one rope with both hands and make circular waves.

- Repeat for desired duration.

Pulleys

24. Kneeling high pulley crunch

- Kneel below a high pulley that contains a rope attachment.
- Grasp cable rope attachment and lower the rope until your hands are placed next to your face.
- Flex your hips slightly and allow the weight to hyperextend the lower back. This will be your starting position.
- With the hips stationary, flex the waist as you contract the abs so that the elbows travel towards the middle of the thighs. Exhale as you perform this portion of the movement and hold the contraction for a second.
- Slowly return to the starting position as you inhale.

25. Reverse cable crunch

- Connect an ankle strap attachment to a low pulley cable. Sit down with your feet towards the pulley and attach the cable to your ankles.
- Lie down, elevate your legs and bend your knees at a 90-degree angle. Your legs and the cable should be aligned.
- With your hands behind your head, bring your knees inwards to your torso and elevate your hips off the floor.
- Pause for a moment, and in a slow and controlled manner, drop your hips and bring your legs back to the starting 90-degree angle. You should still have tension on your abs in the resting position.

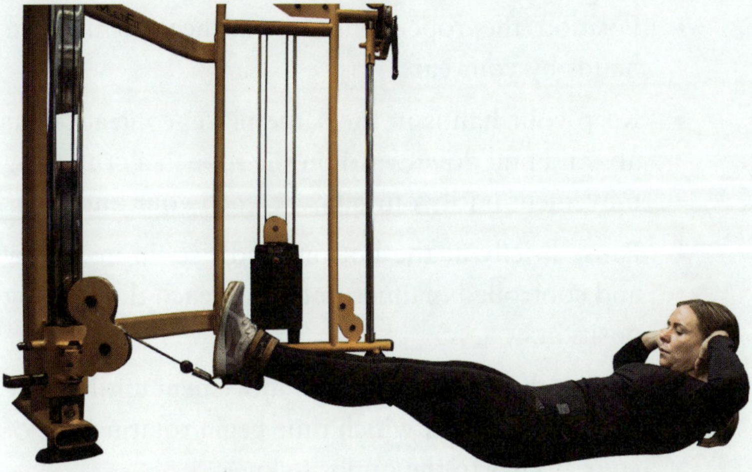

26. Twisting kneeling cable crunch

- Connect a rope attachment to a high pulley cable and position a mat on the floor in front of it.
- Position the rope behind your head with your hands by your ears.
- Keep your hands in the same place, contract your abs and pull downward on the rope in a crunching movement until your elbows reach your knees.
- Pause briefly at the bottom and rise up in a slow and controlled manner until you reach the starting position.
- Repeat the same downward movement until you're halfway down, at which time begin rotating one of your elbows to the opposite knee.
- Again, pause briefly at the bottom and rise up in a slow and controlled manner until you reach the starting position.

- Repeat the same movement as before, but alternate the other elbow to the opposite knee.

Bands

27. Resistance band V sit position hold

- Begin in a seated position with your legs straight and feet on the floor with a resistance band wrapped behind the soles of your feet holding on to either side of the band with your hands.
- Slowly contract your abdominal muscles and core, and lift your legs up to a 45-degree angle raising your feet from the floor.
- It's important to maintain a good core posture and strong spine throughout the movement, and to avoid rounding the shoulders forward.
- Hold this V-shaped position for the desired amount of time. Then relax and repeat.

28. Pall off press

- Set up with a band firmly affixed to an immovable object.

- Stand in a line with the band and turn your body to a perpendicular position. Centre the band on your chest using both hands.
- Push the band straight out in front of you, keeping your body in a straight line with no rotation. Hold it in front for 3 seconds, then return the band in complete control to your chest.
- Repeat for desired number of reps.

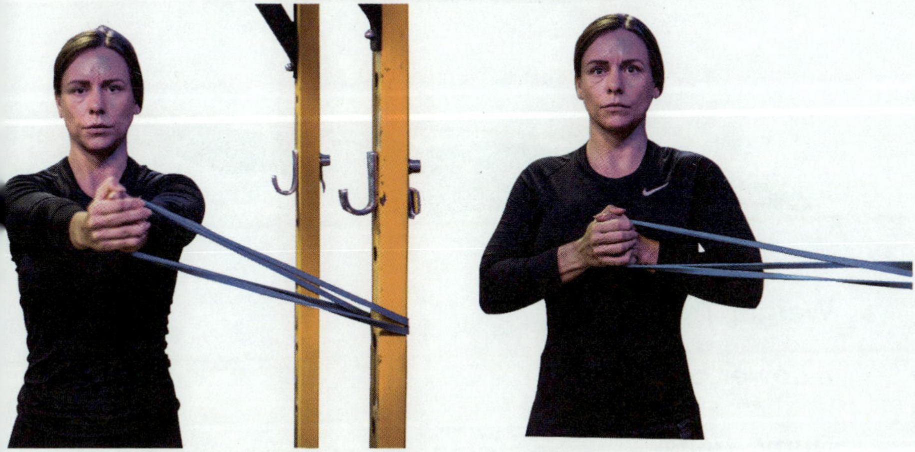

29. Resisted reverse crunch

- Lie on your back on the floor and wrap the resistance band around the arches of your feet.
- Cross the ends of the band over each other to make an 'X' and grasp the ends with opposite hands.
- Bend your hips and knees so that your knees are near your chest and then crunch your torso off the floor. Extend your legs while you raise your arms overhead—keep your shoulder blades off the floor.

- Repeat for desired number of reps.

Weight Training

I. Lower body

Dumb-bells

1. Goblet squats

    - From a standing position, cradle the head of a dumb-bell close to your chest with both hands. You should be looking straight ahead, with your shoulders back, your spine straight, and your feet just outside of shoulder width. This will be your starting position.
    - Initiate the movement by descending into a squat, flexing the hips and knees to lower your body.

Maintain the angle of your torso, paying close attention to the preservation of your spine. As you descend, push your knees outwards and keep your weight on your heels.

- Descend either until you reach the full squat position with your hamstrings on your calves or until your back starts to round. At the bottom of the motion, pause briefly.
- Return to the starting position by driving through your heels, extending the knees and hips to return to the starting position.
- Repeat the movement for the desired number of reps.

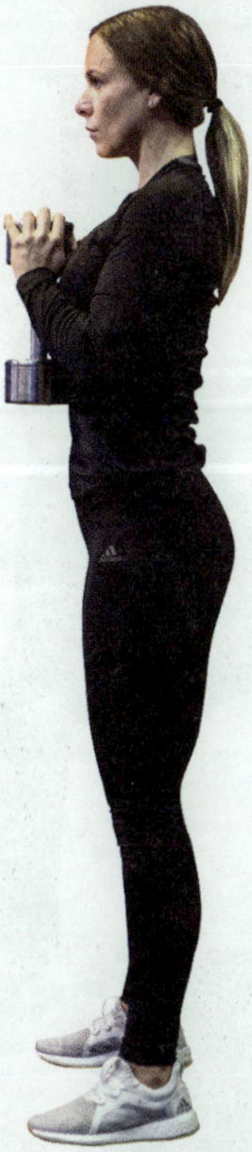

2. **One-legged toe raise**

   - Set up by grasping a dumb-bell in your right hand and standing on the edge of a calf raise block or step with the balls of your feet on the edge.
   - Take your right leg and hook it behind your left.
   - Let your left heel drop as far as possible. This is the starting position.
   - Keeping your body straight and eyes facing forward, raise your left heel up as far as possible.
   - Pause and squeeze the calf muscle, and then slowly lower your heal back down as far as possible.
   - Repeat for desired number of reps, and then do the same with the right leg.

3. **Lateral lunge**

- Stand erect with your feet about shoulder-width apart, holding a pair of dumb-bells together in front of you, palms facing each other.
- Facing forward throughout and staying as upright as possible, take a big step out to your side, angling your foot just slightly out. Descend into a moderately deep squat, keeping your trailing leg straight.
- Push back up and bring your leg back to the start position.
- Repeat on the opposite side and complete the desired number of reps.

4. **Stationary lunge**

    - Stand erect in a split stance holding a pair of dumb-bells in both hands with the palms facing each other.
    - Lower down into a lunge while bending the forward knee to 90 degrees while keeping the chest pushed out and back straight.
    - Hold this position for one second and return to original position.
    - Switch sides and repeat for desired number of reps.

5. **Overhead alternating lunge**

- Stand erect in a split stance, holding two dumbbells overhead with the arms completely locked out.
- Lower down into a lunge while bending the forward knee to 90 degrees while keeping the chest pushed out and back straight.
- Hold this position for one second and return to the original position.
- Switch sides and repeat for desired number of reps.

Med ball

6. **Sumo squat**

    - Stand with your feet slightly more than shoulder-width apart with toes pointed outwards, chest pushed out and back straight.
    - Hold a medicine ball close to your chest, push your hips back and lower down into a squat, maintaining enough tension on the glutes.
    - Hold for one second and return to original position.
    - Repeat for desired number of reps.

7. **Single-leg squat**

- Stand on one leg with your foot pointing straight ahead and your knee slightly bent. Keep your weight centred over the ball of your foot.
- Hold a medicine ball close to your chest.
- Keep your upper body erect with your head facing forward. Tuck your pelvis under and roll your shoulder blades back. Do not round your shoulders.
- Keeping the knee centred over the ball of the foot, lower into a squat position. Once you are at the bottom of the squat raise back up to your starting position.
- Perform a desired number of reps.

8. **Single-leg hip bridge**

    - Lie on the floor with your feet flat and knees bent while keeping a medicine ball close to the chest.
    - Raise one leg off the ground, pulling the knee to your chest. This will be your starting position.
    - Execute the movement by driving through the heel, extending your hip upwards and raising your glutes off the ground.
    - Extend as far as possible, pause and then return to the starting position.

9. **Med ball reverse lunge**

- Start with your feet about hip-width apart, holding a medicine ball in both hands directly in front of your chest.
- Step back into a lunge with both knees in 90-degree angles. Step your back foot back to your front foot.
- Keep your body upright and continue, alternating legs.

Kettlebells

10. Stiff legged deadlift

- Widen your stance to the extent that you can bend over and grab the handle of the kettlebell, while keeping the knees soft.
- Scoot the butt back while bending over, and grab the handle with both hands. Expand the chest and pull the shoulder blades back.
- Leaning back on your heels, and keeping your shins vertical to the ground, exhale, squeeze the glutes, and press the hips forward.

- As you rise into a standing position, continue the chest expansion, and allow the head to drop into neutral alignment with eyes forward.
- Inhale, while reversing the movement. Bend like a hinge, and lower the kettlebell back to the ground.

11. Single-arm overhead kettlebell squat

- Clean and press a kettlebell with one arm. Press the weight overhead by extending through the elbow. This will be your starting position.
- Looking straight ahead and keeping a kettlebell locked out above you, flex the knees and hips and

lower your torso between your legs, keeping your head and chest up.

- Pause at the bottom position for a second before rising back to the top, driving through the heels of your feet.

12. Counter-balance squat

- Hold a kettlebell by its handles, place it in front of your hips and stand with your feet hip-width apart.
- Lower into a squat and simultaneously lift the kettlebell up until your hands are parallel to the floor.
- Hold for one second and return to starting position.
- Repeat for desired number of reps.

13. Single-arm front squat

- Begin by grabbing one kettlebell and placing the bell on top of the forearm. Pull the arm in tight against the chest.
- From there, push the hips back and begin lowering your body as if you were sitting down in a chair.
- Squat between your legs while maintaining a flat back, upright torso and braced abs.
- Push through your heels and return to the starting position.

Sandbag

14. Step up

- Stand up straight while holding a sandbag on your back.
- Place the right foot on the elevated platform. Step on the platform by extending the hip and the knee of your right leg. Use the heel mainly to lift the rest of your body up and place the foot of the left leg on the platform as well. Breathe out as you execute the force required to come up.
- Step down with the left leg by flexing the hip and knee of the right leg as you inhale. Return to the original standing position by placing the right foot next to the left foot on the initial position.

- Repeat with the right leg for the recommended number of repetitions and then move on to doing the same with the left leg.

15. Cannon lunges

- Hold a sandbag with both the attachments and keep it hanging in front, with your feet squared and hip-width apart.
- Perform a reverse lunge by pushing your left leg backwards; simultaneously, rotate and elevate the sandbag to the left shoulder.
- Push the left leg forward and return the sandbag to its original position.
- Switch legs and repeat for desired number of reps.

16. Walking lunges

- Hold the sandbag at chest height, overhead, in a bear hug or any other variation.
- Step forward on one leg.
- Bend both knees and drop your bodyweight downwards until both knees are at 90 degrees.
- Keep the head and chest high throughout.
- Bring your rear leg forward and step through into another lunge.
- Note: Try to avoid resting between lunges—keep the movement smooth and continuous.

17. Lateral step ups

- Stand beside a low box or bench. Hold a sandbag behind the back and keep your chest pushed out.
- Place one foot on to the box or step, keeping your other foot firmly on the floor.
- Press the heel of the foot into the box and drive upwards until your supporting leg becomes completely extended.
- Finish with your trail leg on the box or bench.
- Step down with the trailing leg to return to the starting position.

Tyres

18. Tyre jumps

- Lay your tyre flat on its side like a box. Face the tyre with your feet shoulder-width apart.
- Squat down slightly, as if you are going to jump straight into the air. Your arms will naturally swing backwards and return forward as you leap on to the tyre. Both feet should land softly on the tyre.
- Repeat for desired number of reps.

19. Lateral jumps

- Lay your tyre on its side like a box. Stand perpendicular to the tyre with your feet shoulder-width apart.
- Squat down slightly and leap laterally on to the tyre and land both feet softly on the tyre.
- Repeat for desired number of reps.

20. Toe touches

- Stand facing the tyre, put your hands on the tyre shoulder width apart so you are in a plank position.
- Drive your left knee up and touch the tyre with your toe.
- As your left knee drives up, your right arm will swing back, similar to a running stance.
- Return your left foot to the ground as you drive your right knee up, your left hand back, and your foot to the tyre.
- Repeat for desired number of reps.

21. Pop squats

- Lay the tyre flat on the ground. Stand in the hole in the centre of your tyre.
- Bend your knees slightly and hop upwards to land on the tyre in a 90-degree squat, with both feet on opposite sides of the tyre.
- Hop upwards, returning to a standing position within the hollow of the tyre. This is one repetition.
- Repeat for desired number of reps.

II. Upper body

Dumb-bells

22. Bench press

- Lie down on a flat bench with a dumb-bell in each hand resting on top of your thighs, the palms of your hands facing each other.
- Then, using your thighs to help raise the dumb-bells up, lift the dumb-bells one at a time so that you can hold them in front of you at shoulder width.

- Once at shoulder width, rotate your wrists forward so that the palms of your hands are facing away from you. The dumb-bells should be just to the sides of your chest, with your upper arm and forearm creating a 90-degree angle.

- Then, as you breathe out, use your chest to push the dumb-bells up. Lock your arms at the top of the lift and squeeze your chest, hold for a second and then begin coming down slowly.
- Repeat the movement for the prescribed number of reps.

23. Triceps pushback

- Start with a dumb-bell in each hand and your palms facing your torso.
- Keep your back straight with a slight bend in the knees and bend forward at the waist. Your torso should be almost parallel to the floor. Make sure to keep your head up.
- Your upper arms should be close to your torso and parallel to the floor. Your forearms should be pointed towards the floor as you hold the weights. There should be a 90-degree angle formed between your forearm and upper arm. This is your starting position.
- Now, while keeping your upper arms stationary, exhale and use your triceps to lift the weights until the arm is fully extended. Focus on moving the forearm.
- After a brief pause at the top contraction, inhale and slowly lower the dumb-bells back down to the starting position.

- Repeat for desired number of reps.

24. Hammer curls

- Stand up with your torso upright and a dumb-bell on each hand being held at arm's length. The elbows should be close to the torso.
- The palms of the hands should be facing your torso. This will be your starting position.
- Now, while keeping your upper arms stationary, exhale and curl the weight forward while contracting the biceps. Continue to raise the weight until the biceps are fully contracted and the dumb-bell is at shoulder level. Hold the contracted position for a brief moment as you squeeze the biceps.

- After the brief pause, inhale and slowly begin to lower the dumb-bells back down to the starting position.

25. Bent-over row

- Hold a dumb-bell in each hand with a pronated grip, bend your knees slightly and bring your torso forward by bending at the waist; as you bend, make sure to keep your back straight until it is almost parallel to the floor.
- The weights should hang directly in front of you as your arms hang perpendicular to the floor and your torso. This is your starting position.

- While keeping the torso stationary, lift the dumbbells to your side, keeping the elbows close to the body. On the top contracted position, squeeze the back muscles and hold for a second.
- Slowly lower the weight again to the starting position as you inhale.
- Repeat for the recommended number of reps.

Med balls

26. Med ball plyo push up

- Kneel before the medicine ball. Place your left hand on top of the ball and right hand on the floor, slightly wider than shoulder width away.
- Position your upper body above both hands with the right arm straight and left arm bent with your palm on the ball. Straighten your body with feet on the floor, shoulder-width apart.
- Lower your body until a slight stretch is felt in your shoulder or chest. Immediately, push your body up rapidly. As the right arm straightens and rises above the floor, rapidly roll the ball under the right hand with the left hand.
- Land the right hand on the ball while quickly placing your left hand on the floor, slightly wider than shoulder width.

- Repeat movement with ball under right hand. Continue by alternating between sides.

27. Med ball rolling push up

- Begin in a plank position with right hand on top of medicine ball and left hand on the floor. Hands are directly below shoulders with arms long.
- Begin to lower your chest toward the floor, bending your elbows and keeping the body straight.
- Press up to start position then roll the ball over to the left hand. Repeat the push-up with ball under left hand. This is one repetition.
- Repeat for desired number of reps.

28. Med ball superman

- Lie face down, arms extended in a T, with your right hand on top of the med ball.
- Lift your upper back and feet off the ground a few inches and contract abs into a superman position. From here, pass the ball to the left hand by rolling it in front of you.
- While still holding the superman position, roll ball back to the right hand.
- Repeat.

29. Med ball fly

- Lie face up on a med ball with the neck and shoulder blades resting on the ball's centre, and knees bent at a 90-degree angle.
- With the abs engaged and hips raised, extend the arms, holding a lightweight medicine ball to the ceiling. Shift the ball to the left hand, and slowly

lower the ball until the left arm is parallel with the floor.

- Bring the ball back to the centre and shift the ball to the right hand to complete one rep.
- Repeat for desired number of reps.

Kettlebells

30. Single-arm kettlebell row

- Hold a kettlebell in one hand and stand with your feet in a split stance with the left leg pushed forward.
- Bend with your hips until your back is parallel to the floor, while keeping your back flat.
- Let the kettlebell hang from your right arm while keeping it fully extended.

- Pull the kettlebell towards your stomach while keeping the elbow close to the body.
- Lower your back to the original position and repeat for desired number of reps.

31. Kettlebell pull over

- Lie down on your back, knees bent and feet flat on the ground with the intended weight by your shoulder.
- Press the weight above your chest to straight arms at the elbow; make sure your wrist is not folded backwards.
- Pull your shoulders down and back—make sure you are not shrugging or protracting your shoulders.
- Inhale, brace with your abdomen, and slowly control the weight to just above the ground. If you are lying on a bench, you may take the bell as far back as the overhead position.
- Lift the weight back up to its starting position using your lats, keeping your shoulders down and back.

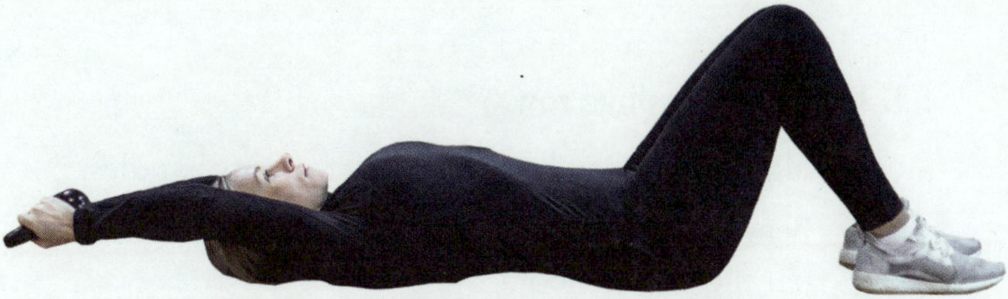

32. **Half-kneeling single-arm press**

- Get yourself into a half-kneeling position with the kettlebell racked on the side where the knee is still on the ground.
- Squeeze the kettlebell and, while keeping your shoulder down, press the bell to a lockout position while maintaining the distance between your ear and bicep.
- Repeat for desired number of reps.

Sandbag

33. Bent-over sandbag row

- Hold a sandbag by grabbing it with its handles.
- Bend with your hips and knees until your back is parallel to the floor.
- Let the sandbag hang in front with a neutral grip.
- Pull the sandbag to your stomach while squeezing the back and keeping the elbows close to the body.
- Return to original position and repeat for desired number of reps.

34. Sandbag clean 'n' press

- Squat down with a straight back and grab the sandbag by the handles.
- In one swift movement, lift the sandbag to your shoulders and sink back down into a squat.
- Push up through your heels and extend your arms to press the sandbag above your head.
- Lower safely to your shoulders and drop back to the floor while maintaining a straight back.
- Repeat for desired number of reps.

Tyres

35. Triceps dips

- Start with your hands close to your hips on the tyre, with legs placed stretched out in front of you.
- Bend your elbows and dip your lower body down. Your butt should graze but not rest on the tyre.
- Return to the original position and squeeze your triceps.
- Repeat for desired number of reps.

36. Decline push ups

- Place your hands shoulder-width apart on the floor and lift your feet on to the tyre so you are in a plank position.
- Lower your upper body, bending your elbows until your chest almost touches the ground, then push back up to the starting position.
- Repeat for desired number of reps.

III Full body

Dumb-bells

37. Dumb-bell snatch

- Using an overhand grip, grab a dumb-bell in one hand and stand with the feet slightly wider than shoulder-width apart.
- Descend your hips to the floor until your knees are bent at 90 degrees, and the dumb-bell is resting on the floor.

- Quickly pull the dumb-bell towards the ceiling while simultaneously extending your knees and hips, and raising your body on the balls of your feet. Keep the dumb-bell close to your body.
- As the dumb-bell reaches its highest point, quickly rotate your elbow under the weight and extend your arm. The dumb-bell will rest over the top of your shoulder with the palm facing away from your body.
- Repeat for desired number of reps.

38. Dumb-bell clean

- Begin standing with a dumb-bell in each hand with your feet shoulder-width apart.
- Lower the weights to the floor by flexing at the hips and knees, pushing your hips back until the dumb-bells reach the floor. This will be your starting position.
- To initiate the movement, violently jump upwards by extending the hips, knees and ankles to accelerate the weights upwards.
- Maintaining a neutral grip on the dumb-bells, keep the arms straight until full extension is reached.
- After full extension, re-bend the hips and knees to receive the weight in a squat position. Allow the arms to bend, guiding the dumb-bells to your shoulders.

- Upon receiving the weight in the squat position, extend the hips and knees to finish in a standing position with the weights on your shoulders.

39. Lunges with curls

- Begin with a dumb-bell held in each hand in an underhand grip. Stand with feet in a split position.
- Lower down into a lunge with both knees bending to 90 degrees and simultaneously flex the elbows and squeeze the biceps.

- Return to original position and repeat for desired number of reps.

40. Stiff leg deadlift with bent-over row

- Hold a dumb-bell in each hand with an overhand grip and stand with feet hip-width apart and toes pointing forward.
- Bend forward from the hips while keeping the knees soft and dumb-bells close to the body. Emphasis should be on keeping the back bent and flat.
- Bend forward, lower and lower till you feel a stretch at the back of your leg. Hold the position for a few seconds and slowly return to your original position.

Med balls

41. Rock 'n' roll up

- Lie down, back on the mat, with your knees bent. Hold a medicine ball on the ground with your arms fully extended overhead.
- Pull the knees into the chest, preparing to use the weight of the ball to help catapult you to a controlled squat position; then stand.
- Slowly lower back into a squat, and ease back to the floor, butt first, before lying back down.

42. **Lunge with overhead press**

- Stand with the feet together, holding a lightweight medicine ball in front of the chest in both hands.
- Lift the right foot off the floor, bending the knee, and hold this position for one count before stepping forward into a lunge.

- With the bodyweight shifting to the right leg, reach the medicine ball straight overhead.
- While still in the lunge, pull the ball back to the chest, and bring the front leg back to the starting position and repeat.

43. Squat press and throw

- Heels grounded, come to a squat position with a medicine ball held close to the chest.
- Drive through the heels to jump, and throw the ball straight up as high as possible.

- Let the ball drop to the ground and repeat.

Kettlebells

44. Clean and press

- Pick up the kettlebell, letting it swing between your legs.

- Keep your upper arm against your side and use a pulling-up motion as if starting a lawn mower.
- Immediately, use an uppercut motion, having the bell end up between your forearm and biceps (this is called the rack position).
- From the rack position, press the kettlebell straight up to lockout and lower the kettlebell back into the rack position.
- Drop the weight smoothly into a swing without jerking your arm.

45. **Kettlebell high pull**

- Place a kettlebell about a foot in front of you.
- With a straight back, grab the handle, swing the kettlebell back and swing it forward forcefully.
- At the top of the motion, quickly pull the kettlebell back keeping it horizontal to the ground.
- Push the kettlebell handle back into the down swing quickly and repeat.

46. Lateral lunge to clean

- Stand with your feet wider than shoulder-width apart and keep a kettlebell hanging on the right side of the body.
- Lower into a lateral lunge by bending the right knee to 90 degrees and keeping the left leg fully extended.
- Return to the original position and keep your upper arm against your side and use a pulling up motion as if starting a lawn mower.
- Immediately, use an uppercut motion having the bell end up between your forearm and biceps.

- Lunge to the other side, and perform a clean again.
- Change hands and repeat for desired number of reps.

Sandbag

47. Front-loaded sandbag good mornings

- Stand with your feet about hip-width apart and hold the sandbag up at your chest with your arms wrapped up around the bag.
- Then hinge over keeping your back flat. As you hinge over, push your butt back and keep your knees soft. Feel a stretch down your hamstrings as you focus on pushing your butt back.
- Make sure to keep your back flat and core engaged. You do not want to feel this move in your low back.
- Drive through your heels to come back up to standing and really squeeze your glutes at the top of the move. Make sure to keep the sandbag up at your chest the entire time.

48. Sandbag squat with alternating shoulder pressing

- Start with your feet shoulder width apart. Hold the middle of the sandbag with both hands. Place it over one shoulder.
- To start press the sandbag up and over your head to the other shoulder. Bring it down to that shoulder, once complete start to squat down and press back up keeping the sandbag on your shoulder.
- Once you are back in your starting position press the sandbag onto the other shoulder, squat down and repeat.
- Keep your core engaged so that you do not feel this move in your low back.

49. Lunge with sandbag halos

- Hold the bag either on both sides or with the handles that allow you to have your palms facing you. Stand with your feet about hip-width to shoulder-width apart and the bag hanging straight down in front of you with your arms straight.
- Then, pull it up to one hip and towards the side of your body. Once you get to the side of your body, start to pull the bag up and back. You are going to pull the bag in a big circle around your upper body and head.

- You will pull up from one hip, towards the outside of your shoulder and then back around behind your head and shoulders before bringing it back outside the other shoulder and around the front to your hips.
- Then, you can either repeat the same circle or switch and go the other direction, bringing it up towards the other hip, outside the shoulder and back around your head and shoulders before returning it back around front.

50. Burpee with upright row

- Start by standing tall with your feet about shoulder-width apart and place two dumb-bells (suitable weight) in either hand. Then bend your knees and squat while bringing your hands to the ground.
- With control, thrust your feet back into a plank position with dumb-bells touching the floor helping support your body. Don't let your hips drop.
- Complete a push-up on the dumb-bells with proper form, then pull your feet forward to meet your hands, and immediately jump straight up off the ground.

- Land softly into a standing position, and raise both dumb-bells making sure elbows pull away from your face and repeat. Hands down with dumb-bells, thrust back, push up on dumb-bells, jump forward, jump up and perform the upright row with the dumb-bells.
- Find a continuous rhythm, and remember to breathe. Perform a certain number of repetitions.

Tyres

51. Tyre flip

- Start with yourself standing tall with feet shoulder width apart. The tyre must be placed in front of you.
- Engage your core and enter a squat position. As you enter the squat position, place your hands underneath the tyre.
- When your hands are firmly placed underneath, lift the tyre by pushing through your heels from the squat position by driving your hips forward and squeezing your buttocks.
- Once you are upright push the tyre through by using full force to ensure the tyre has been flipped.
- Remember to keep your spine neutral and your chest out. Once completed repeat for a desired number of repetitions.

52. Decline push up into knee drive

- Place your hands shoulder-width apart on the floor and lift your feet on to the tyre so you are in a plank position.
- Lower your upper body, bending your elbows until your chest almost touches the ground, then push back up to the starting position.
- As you raise yourself back to the upright position make sure you exhale extending the arms, contracting through the chest. At the top of the movement, make sure you are crunching through your obliques, bringing your knee up to the opposite elbow.
- If you have trouble reaching your elbow, bring the torso forward, making sure your shoulders are in front of your hands. Once you have brought your knee to your chest, relax and repeat with your other knee.

- Carry out the exercise for a preferred amount of repetitions.

IV Core

Dumb-bells

53. **High plank rows**

- Start in a plank position with your hands extended holding on to either dumb-bell on either side.
- As the name suggests you are going to be in a plank with your arms extended fully at your elbows.

- In the plank position, using your left arm pull the dumb-bell up by lifting your arm up making sure that your elbow passes your chest.
- Once you have raised one dumb-bell, release back to the starting position and alternate your arms carrying out the same steps.
- Complete desired number of repetitions.

54. Dumb-bell side bend

- Start this exercise by standing shoulder width apart, standing tall with a neutral spine. Whilst standing straight have a dumb-bell on either side with a natural grip making sure palms are facing your torso.
- Whilst keeping your back straight and your head up, bend only at your waist to the right as far as possible, keeping a tight grip on the dumb-bells. Hold for one second and return to starting position.
- Repeat on either side for desired number of reps.

55. Dumb-bell crunch

- Start this exercise lying on your back with your heels up to your bum.
- With a dumb-bell place your arms so that they are at a 90 degree angle with your body keeping a slight flexion in both elbows.
- Once in the above position, contract your abs and raise your shoulders off the ground so that you are half way between the floor and your knees. Once you are at this points slowly return to the start position and repeat.

56. Dumb-bell superman

- To start this exercise, lie face down on your front with your arms and legs stretched out with the dumb-bells in each of your hands,
- Simultaneously raise your arms out in front of you and your legs behind you making sure they raise off the ground creating a curvature in your lower spine.
- To prevent injury, make sure you keep your head aligned with your spine, squeeze your Gluteus Maximus and Hamstrings and at the same time whilst hyper-flexing your shoulders.
- Hold for 5-10 seconds and return to starting position. Repeat for number of desired repetitions.

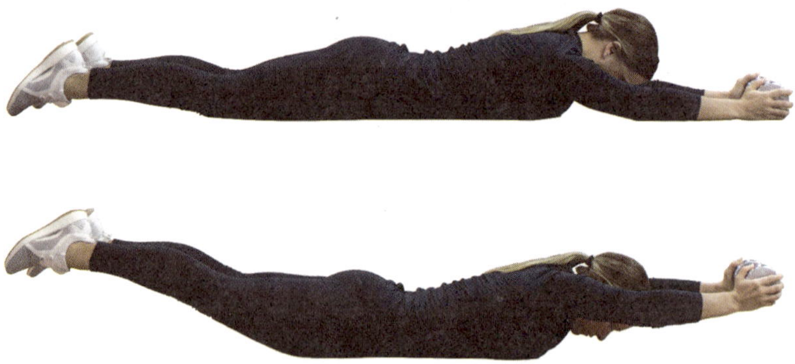

Med balls

57. Med ball high plank

- Starting position is essentially a plank using your hands placed on a medicine ball instead of your forearms
- With the plank you are going to start on your hands and knees, extend your legs straight behind you so that you are in a parallel line from your head position to your feet.
- From here your hands will be placed onto the medicine ball which should be place directly underneath your head/face.
- Hold the plank for a certain amount of time.

58. Med ball rollout

- To start the exercise you need to be on all fours (hands and knees with your arms running parallel to your shoulders, keeping your back flat)
- From the position above, place your hands onto the medicine ball with this directly below your head.
- Next start to roll the medicine ball away from your body keeping your core engaged and spine straight. Extend out with the ball as far as possible before you lose control and technique, once you are at your limit, start to roll the ball back towards you back to the start position
- This is a slow and controlled movement, complete the desired number of reps.

59. Transverse med ball throws

- The Transverse medicine ball throw is also known as a 'Lateral' medicine ball throw and is a great core stability exercise which also uses a lot of power.
- To start with, you will need to find a stable wall or a person to throw the ball against or too, from there, stand with your feet just wider than shoulder width apart to create a strong and stable base
- Now make sure that either your left or right shoulder is pointing towards the wall/partner. If you are stood with your left shoulder facing the wall, start with the medicine ball by your right hip.
- Your first movement should be the rotation with your hips as powerful as possible, the rotation of the hips will create a 'lag' in your arms, you can use this lag with your core to create a powerful throw and release of the medicine ball against the wall or person.
- Once let go, you can either catch the ball and restart, or let the fall to the floor and restart the exercise process.
- Complete this exercise for the desired number of reps.

Kettlebells

60. Kettlebell swing

- Stand tall, still gripping the kettlebell. Keep your arms long and loose while squeezing shoulders blades together and engaging your core.
- Driving through your heels, explode through hips to send weight swinging upwards from quads. Aim for chest height, with arms extended.
- As the kettlebell begins to descend, let the weight do the work as you ready your body for the next rep. Shift weight back into heels while hinging at the hips and loading both the hamstrings and glutes. Receive the weight, allowing the kettlebell to ride back between legs.

- As it makes the transition backwards to forward, drive through the heels and hips to repeat.

61. Kettlebell windmills

- Place a kettlebell in front of your lead foot and clean and press it overhead with your opposite arm. Clean the kettlebell to your shoulder by extending through the legs and hips as you pull the kettlebell towards your shoulders. Rotate your wrist as you do so, so that the palm faces forward. Press it overhead by extending the elbow.
- Keeping the kettlebell locked out at all times, push your butt out in the direction of the locked-out kettlebell.

- Turn your feet out at a 45-degree angle from the arm with the locked out kettlebell.
- Bending at the hip to one side and sticking your butt out, slowly lean until you can touch the floor with your free hand.
- Keep your eyes on the kettlebell that you hold over your head at all times.
- Pause for a second after reaching the ground and reverse the motion back to the starting position.

62. Kettlebell renegade row

- Place two kettlebells a little closer than shoulder-width apart and get into the push-up position on top of the kettlebells holding on to the handles.
- Keep your body as straight as possible from your head to your toes.
- Press into the ground as hard as you can with your left hand and foot, and pull up with your right.
- Lower the kettlebell back down and alternate sides, now pulling up with your left hand.

Sandbag

63. Sandbag pulls

- Set up in a plank position from your hands and toes or hands and knees, and place the sandbag on the ground to one side of your body just outside and below your shoulder.
- Make sure your hands are under your shoulders; you may want to set your feet or knees wider apart to give you more stability.
- Reach one hand under your body and across to grab the sandbag.
- Squeeze your glutes and, without rotating your hips, pull the sandbag through and across to the other side of your body.
- Then reach through with the other hand to pull it back.
- Repeat for desired number of reps.

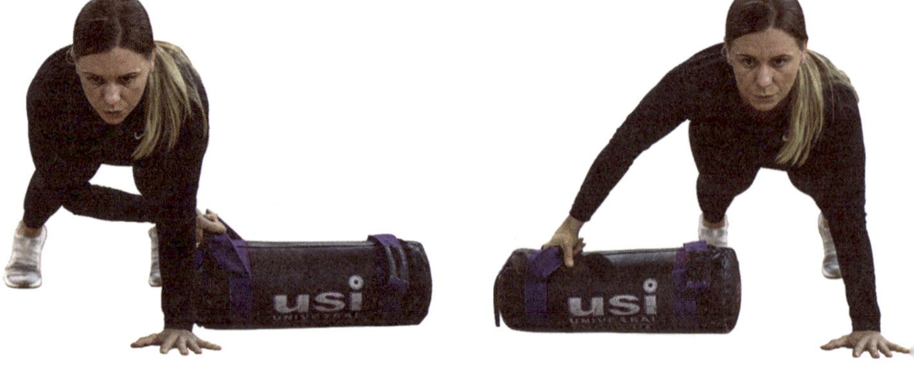

64. Wood chops

- Start by standing with your feet shoulder-width apart and your knees slightly bent holding a sandbag at about knee level to one side of your body.
- Slowly bring the sandbag in a diagonal direction, raising it over your head and shoulders, squeezing your oblique muscles.
- Return to the starting position and repeat for as many reps and sets as desired.

65. Sandbag shouldering

- Place a sandbag in between your feet and grab it around the middle with both hands. Sink your butt and hinge forward so you are in a conventional deadlift position.
- Then squeeze your glutes and stand up, swinging the sandbag up and over one shoulder.
- Keep your back flat as you swing the sandbag up and squeeze your glutes at the top of the motion.
- Then lower the bag back down to the ground and repeat, swinging the bag up over the other shoulder.
- You can choose to alternate shoulders or complete all reps to one side before switching.

Tyres

66. Sledgehammer hits

- Stand in front of the tyre about 2 feet away from it with a staggered stance. Grip the sledgehammer.
- If you are right-handed, your left hand should be at the bottom of the handle, and your right hand should be choking up closer to the head.
- As you bring the sledge up, your right hand slides towards the head; as you swing down, your right hand will slide down to join your left hand.
- Slam it down as hard as you can against the tyre.
- Control the bounce of the hammer off the tyre.
- Repeat on the other side.

67. Farmer's walk

- Stand inside a tyre with the palms of your hands inverted out.
- Lift the tyre in a deadlift and stand tall with your back straight, shoulder blades retracted and core engaged.
- Walk in a straight line for 10 steps and lower the tyre to the ground in a deadlift.
- You can choose the length to which you want to carry the tyre.

68. **Tyre deadlift**

- Stand with your feet hip-width apart inside a tyre.
- Bend at your hips and knees, and grab the tyre in an inverted grip while keeping the back flat.
- Drive with your glutes and extend the hip till you are standing straight.
- Lower the tyre and repeat for desired number of reps.

V Abdomen

Dumb-bells

69. Renegade row

- Place two dumb-bells on the floor about shoulder-width apart. Start at the top position of the push-up position with your hands on the weights.
- Row one weight up towards the side of your body while balancing on your other hand and feet.
- Hold for one second at the top and return the weight slowly to the starting position to repeat on the other side.

70. Dumb-bell twists

- Sit on the floor with your knees bent and feet elevated.
- Hold a dumb-bell vertically in front of your chest, and lean back so that your torso is at a 45-degree angle to the floor.
- Turn your torso to the left, pause, and squeeze your abs muscles. Return to centre.
- Repeat to the right side, and return to centre.
- Repeat for desired number of reps.

Med balls

71. Med ball smashes

- Hold a med ball with both hands and stand with your feet shoulder-width apart. This will be your starting position.
- Initiate the countermovement by raising the ball above your head and fully extending your body.
- Reverse the motion, slamming the ball into the ground directly in front of you as hard as you can.
- Receive the ball with both hands on the bounce and repeat the movement.

Kettlebells

72. Kettlebell V-hold

- Begin in a seated position with your legs straight and feet on the floor with a kettlebell held close to your chest.

- Slowly contract your abdominal muscles and core, and lift your legs up to a 45-degree angle raising your feet from the floor.
- It's important to maintain a good core posture and strong spine throughout the movement, and to avoid rounding the shoulders forward.
- Hold this V-shaped position for the desired amount of time. Then relax and repeat.

73. Kettlebell Russian twists

- Sit on the floor with your knees bent and feet elevated.
- Hold a kettlebell with the horns in front of your chest, and lean back so that your torso is at a 45-degree angle to the floor.
- Turn your torso to the left, pause, and squeeze your abs muscles. Return to centre.
- Repeat to the right side, and return to centre.

Sandbag

74. Kneeling press outs

- Position yourself in a kneeling position with the back straight, shoulder blades retracted and core braced, holding a sandbag vertically close to the chest.

- Push the sandbag forward and extend the elbows completely.
- Return to the original position and repeat for desired number of reps.

In a nutshell

- Functional training replicates real-life scenarios so that you can perform your daily chores effectively, without getting tired, and at the same time feel fit. It is fitness for life. It also helps train sportspersons and athletes whose functional movements are multidirectional and rotational, and certainly not in a single plane as is done through conventional training equipment.
- Functional fitness training does not rely too much on equipment. It can be divided into three basic blocks:

training using body weight; training using bands, pulleys and battle ropes; and training using other equipment like medicine balls and kettlebells.

- We have explained above exercises under each of the three blocks. There could, however, be various iteration in the exercises mentioned.
- We have also given you sufficient input on each of the important functional training equipment. Specifically, we have covered the following in this chapter:
    - Exercises using body weight without equipment
    - Exercises using battle ropes, pulleys and bands
    - Exercises using dumb-bells and kettlebells
    - Exercises using medicine balls and softballs
    - Exercises using sandbags
- Specific description of every equipment, its size, history and use has been given in detail. If you are getting into a fitness programme, it will be good to understand these basics.

While functional training can happen outside of gyms, they can prove to be essential for sustained change in body and mind outlook. Gyms are like places of worship. They have the same impact on those exercising in them, as temples do on people who pray there together. Gyms are great venue in which to socialize too.

6

Criterion for Effective Training

> 'Fitness is not about being better than someone else ... It's about being better than you used to be.'
>
> —Khloe Kardashian

FUNCTIONAL TRAINING AS such takes care of the physical fitness required by anyone who wants to remain fit, lean and healthy. Since it deals with the 'functions' that we perform, it also takes care of fitness for sportsmen and athletes whose needs go beyond body- and muscle-building exercises that conventional training focuses on. Yet, it would be prudent to say that somebody may like to mix and match functional training and conventional weight training to suit his personal requirements. Therefore, there is no hard and fast rule or researched information that confirms that both cannot go hand in hand and side by side too. Alternatively, a person may first follow functional training methodology for the initial days of his training and later switch over to conventional training, or vice versa.

Many athletes combine several methods and undertake several different training approaches that work best for them. There are also top players and athletes who have achieved top performance on the sheer basis of their talent and therefore did minimal training. Simply put, in training and physical fitness, one size *does not* fit all.

Our experience, which is not limited to functional training alone, also confirms this. Training thousands of people, including the trainers, in functional training for years has convinced us that if done sincerely and with the guidance of trainers, functional training will take care of all that you need to remain fit as a fiddle, and help you in any sport or athletic activity you may be preparing for. Don't treat fitness as an event-based activity (preparing for a wedding or a beauty contest; and make it a lifetime companion.

How do we benchmark physical training?

If a training regimen gives you no pain while exercising, has biomechanical specificity, has good control and form, improves your 'feel fit' feeling, enhances your quality of movement and effectiveness in what you do for a living, and also improves this on a week to week basis, it is an effective training programme.

Let us look at some basic markers that tell us that we are on the right track and are doing the right kind of training.

1. Pain-free workouts

Pretty basic, but this is important. Here, 'no pain no gain' does not apply. In fitness programmes, or while doing any physical activity, pain acts like a defence mechanism. It tells you that something is not right and is a signal to 'stop right now'. If you don't listen to your body's signals you could land up with some permanent or serious problem with any of your muscles, bones or ligaments.

2. Training specificity

Your body is a fabulous creation of nature because it is highly adaptable. You keep loading one part of the body and it becomes stronger and stronger. But the reverse is also true. If you put your right arm in a Plaster of Paris (POP) cast, which is done for a fractured bone, that arm is out of action for six to eight weeks and in a rest position for that long. Muscles and joints don't move at all. Once the plaster is removed, you will notice that there is hardly any energy in the muscles and you can't even move your arm, let alone lifting any weight. The muscles that have been trapped for a very long time with no exercise have become weak. So when you start exercising them with weights, slings and with the help of a therapist, you gradually revive the arm and bring it back to normal.

This clarity on what you want out of physiotherapy is specificity because you are specific as to what is required from the exercises that the physiotherapist has to prescribe. The definition of specificity is 'the quality of belonging or relating uniquely to a particular subject'.

How does this connect with functional training or physical training? The specificity principle in functional fitness explains that the human body will adapt specifically to the demands placed upon it. It translates into being specific towards what is desired as an outcome from an organized fitness effort.

Metabolic specificity

This refers to the training adaptations gain from working the different energy systems during your workout. It could be excelling in short spurts of vigorous exercise (a game of squash, or a 100-metre sprint). Here you are pushing your anaerobic system. Or it could be longer bouts of sub-maximal exercise, say a 10-km run which will load your aerobic energy systems the most, leading to you being able to perform better at lower-intensity, longer duration efforts.

Biomechanical specificity

This is how your body responds and adapts to resistance training and weights. This helps in identifying exercises to improve and strengthen one specific area of your body, say biceps or shoulder muscles. One can appreciate a negative adaptation with yoga. Some yogasanas are designed to put reverse pressure on certain body parts, in the opposite direction of what you normally do. We always either keep our spine straight bent forward most of the time. Yoga reverses this with certain *asanas*. The *Bhujang Asana* is a case in point, which bends your spine backwards, something we seldom do. This helps to unwind the spine and connected muscles. This exercise is very effective in relieving and even eliminating back pain or such related problems. Yogasanas make your body supple and strong. Yoga practitioners do not have bulging muscles, yet they are very agile and fit.

Psychological specificity

This relates to mental effort and intent and tenacity. It simply translates to: 'when the going gets tough, the tough get going'. If you consciously work towards something, with focused attention and a strong resolve, you will definitely build tenacity and a strong will power. When one goes through military training, especially the commando training, the course appears to be 'all physical', but at the end of it you realize that it is more to do with a mental makeup and will power. You say, 'Oh, I did it, and I can do it again'. If you were successful once doing a 40-km run with a 25 kg backpack and a rifle, you are sorted for life. If ever a situation arises in the future, in a battlefield or otherwise, to run 40 km with your weapon in hand, there will be a 'total recall' of your earlier experience and 'yes, I did it and I can' will flash through your head, giving you that badly required adrenalin to move on. It will give you confidence that this is possible for you.

When you join a gym, it changes your fitness quotient and boosts your confidence. You not only are fit but you also feel fit, and both are important. You appear more confident wherever you go and whatever situation you are in.

Testing specificity

Here you specify targets and achievements. PFTs are physical fitness tests which are used extensively for fitness. You may be required to do a 10-mile run in a particular timeframe, or 30 push-ups at a stretch to pass a test. You might be asked to do a certain number of chin-ups to achieve the target or meet the passing criterion. Similarly, there are specific tests to measure your progress in training.

3. Coordination and control

This is yet another criterion to determine whether you are on the right track. You should never do a physical training, swimming or play any game in an inappropriate manner. Let us explain this. In swimming, if you do not learn a stroke correctly, you will pick up a wrong style due to which you will never be able to achieve your targeted speed, the number of laps you desire to do, and will get exhausted much earlier than you should. The same applies to every game or sport. That is why coaches and trainers are required to constantly correct you and mentor you so that you develop a correct style. Golf is a case in point. It is so technical and sophisticated that without a coach you should never try to learn this game. Even the most seasoned players and professionals take coaching every now and then to get a check on their stance, the swing or the positioning of the ball, position of shoulders and bending of the back or knees, etc. This is not only true for golf, its true for other sports as well, a classical example is cricket where batsmen go to practice pitches where they work on their own area of improvement and try to rework on incorrect muscle memories.

Similarly, one should not learn yoga by watching a video lesson online. First learn it from an expert, pick up the correct postures, learn every asana and only then attempt to practise it on your own.

Keeping this criterion in mind, you must focus on the appropriateness and correctness of every motion, every movement and every exercise that you undertake while working out. Insist on correctness and go by the book—it will go a long way in achieving what you have set out to do.

In our daily life we take a wrong posture while sitting, thus overloading a few muscles all the time. This leads to problems like spondylitis or back pain or the neck muscles being overworked, thereby causing stiffness.

4. *Gradual progress*

Steady progress demonstrates that you are doing the right things and doing them right. This is true for every field. In studies, you work hard and that reflects in the marks you score. If you are studying hard and not scoring, something is wrong, and you need to look at how you study. If you are coaching for cricket but your scores are not going up and you are not getting the desired flow of shots , then there is something wrong—you either need to be more attentive while getting coached or change the coach.

In fitness, progress can be measured in different ways. It could be heavier weights as you keep exercising over a period of time, more reps in less time, speed, power, less pain and fatigue, and so on. For functional fitness, it is difficult to put down on paper how you are progressing on different parameters. For instance, stability is difficult to measure in definite terms.

Patience and perseverance are key for progress. Sometimes you may make quick progress in the first two weeks of training and then hit a plateau and begin to feel that you are not progressing. This can happen in weight loss programmes too. First three weeks, you shed a lot of fat, and then you hit a wall and observe no progress for the next two weeks. Actually, in fitness, lack of progress is because of lack of patience. You want quick results and that may not be as per your satisfaction and yet you want to move on to more advanced exercises or reach higher speed, flexibility or take on more load.

A better way is to remain focused, not expect miracles, give yourself time and not be overambitious. Rule of thumb should be that you first master an exercise before you take on the more difficult one.

These are the parameters that broadly indicate that you are on the right lines and your effort is not being wasted. Doing it wrong is like a boiler which has a leak—most of the steam goes waste!

Now let us show you how to ramp up or ramp down any exercise. By using the same weight for instance, you can change the degree of difficulty by using different techniques and different methods. We will discuss a few of them now.

Optimization

We can bring variations to exercises and use of training equipment to either make the exercise more strenuous or make it easier to perform. It is logical that as one progresses there is a need to push yourself to move to the next notch and that is what we described as steady progression earlier on. Sounds simple, but it needs to be understood well. Let us now examine different ways of making exercises more and more difficult (or easy) by employing different techniques.

Take a pair of 3-kg dumb-bells and lift each with one hand. Now keep your arms straight down the side of your body, palms facing inwards. Raise both dumb-bells until your wrist is in line with your shoulders, elbows bent and the lower arm perpendicular to the ground, and slowly bring them down to original position. This is the most basic exercise for strengthening your biceps.

Now using the same dumb-bells, try this: Hold the dumb-bells, each arm down the sides of your body. Now move the arms outwards, stretching them, palms facing the ground.

It is much more difficult than the first one where you were bending your arms at the elbows giving you advantage of a short lever. In this case, your arms are straight, and holding the same weight becomes more strenuous. Keeping your arms in horizontal position with weight for even a few seconds is difficult.

Let us look at simple push-ups where you are on all fours, palms near your shoulders. It is by far the most basic exercise. Now do this putting your hands on the bench. This is easier than doing it from the floor because the push-up from floor gives you longest lever arm from the feet on the floor and this becomes shorter when your hands are on bench. When you put your knees on the ground with hands on the floor, then too you are shortening the lever arm making the push-ups easier.

Changing speed

As a rule of thumb, whenever you increase speed, your exercise becomes more difficult. But in exercises like cycling, jogging, walking, doing bicep curls with dumb-bells, etc., slower speed makes the exercise more difficult. For example, doing bench press if you move the arms in and out faster may be easier than doing this slowly. In the slower movement, strain and resistance for muscles is more than in the faster one.

Varying the support base

Using a kettlebell and doing bicep curls standing on two legs is much easier than doing it standing on one leg. Increasing the support base gives you more stability. Doing push-ups with one arm is so difficult that very few attempt it. Here again, the base of support is reduced.

Adding more weight

This is a no-brainer. As you progress and are comfortable with certain sets of weights, you can notch it up by increasing the weight. But this needs to be done gradually to avoid injury.

In a nutshell

- Functional fitness in general makes you fit to lead a healthy life and develop a healthy body. It also takes care of the requirement of people who are into sports and athletes.
- Functional training takes care of all fitness requirements, yet people do a mix and match and add conventional exercises, like weight training and jogging.
- It is essential to ensure that the training you undertake is the right one and it will give you results, else you would just be wasting time, money and effort. A wholesome training that is right must have some essentials: it should give you no pain while exercising, have biomechanical specificity, have good control and form, improve your 'feel fit' feeling and quality of movement and effectiveness, and do this on a week to week basis.
- Four essentials of an appropriate training are specificity, painless exercises, coordination and control, and gradual improvement.
- The training specificity principle says that the human body will adapt specifically to the demands placed

upon it, or specific adaptations to imposed demands. It translates into being specific towards what is desired as an outcome from an organized fitness effort.

- Coordination and control means that you must perform every exercise as per the book and as explained by the coach. Doing it wrong will land you with little results and may cause injury.
- Training should never be painful. If an exercise causes undue pain, it means that the body is giving you feedback that there is something wrong. Proper training will never hurt you or cause injury.
- Every training programme undertaken must yield results progressively. If you are doing things right then you must be able to see the results, else you need to ask yourself what is wrong. Here your coach can help you.
- Once you are comfortable with what you are doing you should move to the next level, recalibrate your goal. You may increase weights, add more speed and rotation to your exercises and even use different ways as explained in this chapter to keep making things more and more challenging. This needs to be done gradually—slowly but surely.

7

Rifle Workout

'The deadliest weapon in the world is a marine and his rifle!'

—John J. Pershing, US General of the Armies

RIFLE WORKOUT, A staple exercise for the armed forces, is a great exercise for anyone who wants to remain fit and agile. This can be easily adapted to and included in any functional fitness programme.

A footballer does not dribble only with a football; he can dribble pretty well with whatever comes his way—a cricket ball, a tennis ball, a softball or even a tin can on the road. A good cricket fielder or a baseball player can catch not only a cricket ball but also a coke bottle or a stone or a bunch of keys thrown at him. A hockey player can manage to handle any round object with a hockey stick and dribble it for fun sake.

Swordsmen in earlier days of combat were very good at handling their swords, which were heavy and sharp. They used to practise for hours on end, either with a partner or with a dummy. They would also practise with sticks the same tactics and moves that are used in sword fight. The idea was to get as comfortable with a sword as possible.

For a soldier, his rifle is an indispensable item of his kit. In battle, it is his only reliable companion. He carries it all the time, everywhere he goes.

Rifle workout makes a soldier comfortable with his weapon of choice, and it is also a great exercise to build strength and endurance. It is done by using dummy guns, which in earlier days were crafted out of wood. Now replicas of all sorts of weapons are available using extremely durable urethane-based materials. The idea is to use the inexpensive dummies so as to avoid wear and tear to actual weapons which are very expensive. The most popular weapon is a rifle, and different personal weapons have different weights, shapes and sizes.

Most rifles weigh around 3.5–5 kg without a loaded magazine. The dummy rifles are available in the range of 4–5 kg and are designed to withstand high-impact usage in the open ground or a well laid out gym.

Rifle exercises are conditioning exercises excellent for exercising arms, shoulders and back muscles. These mainly concentrate on the upper body, but squats that are required for practising firing positions do exercise the leg muscles too.

Exercise 1: Fore up, behind back

Exercise 2: Lunge side, turn and bend

Exercise 3: Fore up, Back bend

Exercise 4: Up and forward

Exercise 5: Fore up, full squat

Exercise 6: Simple bicep curls wit rifle in both hands

Exercise 7: Simple Biceps curls with one arm and hand

Nutrition

IT'S NOT THE 1 hour in the gym that's difficult; it's the other 23 hours!

Introduction

For decades humans' food habits, food patterns, food cultivation and food quality have been evolving. In the twenty-first century, with the drastic change in lifestyle over the past decade, there is now hardly any physical activity throughout the day, sleep is interrupted, stress levels are very high and easily available food options that are mostly unhealthy and junk have replaced the healthy homemade food, because people no longer have the time or patience to cook. With food joints at every nook and corner serving processed, packed and fried foods, the health of the average person has deteriorated drastically. And the increase of obesity along with various other diseases has been exponential. Therefore, nutrition science has become the call of the day because a healthy and balanced diet can prevent many metabolic disorders and diseases which otherwise ail most people. Basic nutrition is all about understanding the nutrients that food provides to our body.

The most commonly neglected thing that out body needs is water. The body requires water in large amounts for all the chemical reactions to be performed, which makes water equally important to the other nutrients. Water, unlike other macronutrients, doesn't give any energy to the body, but aids various processes in the body.

Carbohydrates, proteins and fats, also known as the macronutrients, provide energy to the body. They are called macronutrients because our body needs them in large quantities. These macronutrients, combined with micronutrients, play a vital role in survival, growth, health and bodily functions.

Vitamins and minerals are the micronutrients. Our body needs these micronutrients in small amounts; that's why they are called micronutrients. If any one of them is lacking in our daily food intake, it has its own consequences and side effects on our health.

Therefore, good nutrition plays an important role in our well-being, strengthening the immune system, keeping us energetic, maintaining our psychological wellbeing, etc. All these nutrients together are like fuel for the body's engine. That means they provide energy to the body or play a crucial role in helping the body perform well. Energy derived from food is generally measured in calories.

What Is Good Nutrition?

Good nutrition basically is a balanced diet which daily provides all the macronutrients and micronutrients to the body in the required amounts. Good nutrition practices not only will lead to a healthier life but also to a disease-free body. Whereas bad nutrition is a diet that lacks in one or more essential nutrients and is calorie-dense food consumption which will lead to many nutritional deficiencies, obesity, diseases and disorders.

Understanding Nutrients in Detail

1. Carbohydrates

When carbohydrates are digested in our body, the end form is glucose. Body uses glucose as the primary energy source. 1 gram of carbohydrate gives 4 kcal of energy to the body. Glucose, once it is released in the blood stream, can be utilized immediately if needed, though there are a few storage sites of unused glucose as well. The body stores glucose in the form of glycogen in the muscles and the liver, and in adipose tissue in the form of fats. Therefore, intake of carbohydrates should be according to the daily requirement and one shouldn't overdo it. Apart from being the primary fuel for the body, carbs also spare muscle mass from being used for energy; that is, in the absence of carbohydrates, the body burns muscular proteins to produce energy, which leads to muscle loss. To prevent this, enough carbohydrate consumption should be there in the diet. Hence, carbs are critical for the body. There are different types of carbohydrates and their sources. Some are healthy, and should be included in the diet. Some are unhealthy, and so should be used sparingly included in the diet. These are:

- **Simple carbohydrates:** Simple carbohydrates are refined sugars that score very less on the nutrient index but are caloric-dense. Simple carbohydrates also spike blood sugar levels and very rapidly at that. A consistent spike in blood sugar levels will lead to health complications like insulin resistance, diabetes, metabolic disorders, obesity, etc. Sources of these carbohydrates are refined flours, table sugar, packaged food, etc.
- **Complex carbohydrates:** Complex carbohydrates, unlike simple sugars, spike blood sugar levels gradually, which doesn't let glucose get converted to fat that might get deposited in the body. Complex carbohydrates are also packed with vitamins and minerals and fibres, which has an additional benefit on the body. Sources of these are: whole grains like wheat, jowar and bajra, brown rice, oats, quinoa, as well as pulses and lentils, etc.
- **Fibre:** Fibre is the indigestible part of plant foods that travels through our digestive system, absorbing water along the way and easing bowel movements. Thus, it helps in relieving constipation. Fibres don't get absorbed in the body; therefore they are generally known as roughage. A high-fibre intake contributes towards weight loss as well. Fibre produces a feeling of fullness without adding calories to the total intake. This can help prevent overeating and binge eating, and consequently overweight/obesity. Fibre-rich foods, however, (such as vegetables and fruits, cereals and pulses) are a great source of vitamins and minerals.

2. Proteins

Being one of the irreplaceable macronutrients, proteins are the molecules made of chains of amino acids that our cells require to function. There are such 20 amino acids. The structure and function of our bodies depend on proteins. Muscles, skin, bones and other parts of the human body contain significant amounts of protein, including enzymes and hormones. Therefore, the regulation and function of the body's cells, tissues and organs cannot happen without them. Proteins are also used as the secondary energy source in case of unavailability of carbohydrates. 1 g of protein gives 4 kcal of energy.

Protein has a role to play in the growth and development of a living being. There are parameters that determine the protein requirement of an individual. Some of these parameters are age, illness, pregnancy, physical activity level and health.

Enzymes are proteins that aid a number of biochemical reactions that take place within and outside the cells in the body. Enzymes carry out bodily functions such as digestion, energy production, blood clotting, muscle contraction, etc. In case of insufficiency of proteins, it can lead to these functions being affected—leading to different disorders.

Hormones such as sex hormones, growth hormones, insulin, glucagon, etc., are protein in nature. Unavailability of proteins will lead to many health complications for it being so widely used in the body and having a role in many important functions.

Protein also provides structure to the body as it is present in various structures like bones and skin in the form of collagen, skin and hair in the form of keratin, etc.

Apart from these, it also plays a role in pH balance, fluid balance, immunity health and transport and storage of nutrients.

There are types of proteins depending on the amino acids present in it. These are:

- **Complete proteins**: This group is also called the first-class protein sources. These foods contain all the essential amino acids. They are mostly present in animal foods, such as meats, dairy products, and eggs.
- **Incomplete proteins**: These foods are deficient in at least one essential amino acid, so there is a lack of balance in the proteins. E.g., plant protein sources, peas, lentils, pulses, cereals, nuts, etc.
- **Complementary proteins**: These are a combination of two incomplete proteins taken together in such a way that it completes the amino acid score, thereby enhancing the absorption of the protein. E.g., dal with rice, roti with sprouts, etc.

3. Fats

Just as not all carbohydrates are healthy, not all fats are unhealthy. Our body needs daily dietary intake of fats to keep it going. Hence, fat is another irreplaceable macronutrient in the diet as it provides fat-soluble vitamins A, D, E and K to the body as well as essential fatty acids that are required for healthy heart, skin, bone and hair. Fats are of four types: saturated, monounsaturated, polyunsaturated and trans fats. Advisable sources of fat from each group can be: coconut oil, ghee, butter, milk, curd, cheese, cottage cheese for the saturated fatty acids; avocado, nuts and olive oil for monounsaturated fatty acids; omega-3 fatty acids from the polyunsaturated fats the sources of which are fish like salmon, mackerel, flaxseeds, etc. These type of fatty acids play a major role in controlling body temperature, that is, thermoregulation, which also has a role in protecting the cell membranes of the cells. Consumption of these will prevent arthritis whereas deficiency of these in the body can cause growth retardation, night blindness, anaemia and a poor immunity system. Apart from these functions, fats, just like carbohydrates, are used for energy production. They provide 9 kcal of energy per 1 gram. They are also the largest energy storage form in the body.

The last type of fats—which is trans fatty acids/ hydrogenated fats—are the unhealthiest ones because of the chemical properties they possess. Trans fats are known to cause health issues like chronic heart diseases, insulin resistance, type-2 diabetes, stroke, inflammation, increased triglycerides in blood, etc. They harm your body even if taken in smaller amounts. They come from processed and packed foods, bakery products like cookies and pastries, fried foods, and junk foods like pizzas, burgers and French fries. Therefore, this group should be completely avoided.

4. Water

A human body is made up of 60–70 per cent water. Therefore water is a vital and essential nutrient. Deprivation of water, also called dehydration, can lead to numerous health issues, such as dizziness, fatigue, muscle cramps, temperature irregularities, etc. Severe dehydration can even lead to death. The body loses water through different ways such as through various chemical reactions, sweating, digesting food, breathing, etc. Therefore, consuming water frequently is a need for the body. Some of the various functions water performs are:

- Regulates body temperature
- Protects body organs and tissues
- Helps prevent constipation
- Acts as a solvent to carry nutrients and make them accessible to the body
- Flushes toxins out, thus, keeping the body detoxified
- Lubricates joints
- Moistens tissues in the mouth, nose and eyes
- Maximizes physical performance
- Aids in digestion and nutrient absorption
- Improves blood oxygen circulation
- Helps boost energy and skin health

5. Vitamins

Vitamins are nutrients your body needs to function and prevent and cure disease. They are as important as macronutrients in the growth and development of living beings. To avoid vitamin deficiency, one must consume a variety of food items periodically. Few vitamins have some toxic effects if they are taken in larger amounts than what the body requires—though vitamin toxicity is seen very rarely. There are 13 vitamins that the body needs. They are divided into two types:

- Fat-soluble vitamins: Fat soluble vitamins are transported and absorbed with the help of fats. They are absorbed from the intestinal tract. They have storage sites in the fatty tissues in the human body. These vitamins are vitamin A, D, E and K.
- Water-soluble vitamins: These vitamins dissolve easily in water and are easily excreted. These vitamins have no storage sites in the body; thus, they need to be taken on a daily basis through the food in required amount. Vitamin C and B-complex vitamins which are thiamine (vitamin B1), riboflavin (vitamin B2), niacin (vitamin B3), pantothenic acid (vitamin B5), pyridoxine (vitamin B6), biotin (vitamin B7), folic acid/folate (vitamin B9) and vitamin B12.

To understand the importance and functions of vitamins and their deficit symptoms, refer to the table below:

Nutrient	Function	Sources	Deficiency symptoms
Fat-soluble vitamins			
Vitamin A	Promotes healthy vision and skin. Supports bone and teeth growth. Plays a role in the immune system and reproductive functions.	Green, red, orange, yellow fruits and vegetables, dairy products, organ meat and liver, fish oil.	Xerophthalmia—drying of the cornea; night blindness; dry, flaky skin.

Nutrient	Function	Sources	Deficiency symptoms
Vitamin D	Helps body absorb calcium; therefore, essential for normal bone and tooth development.	Synthesized when skin is exposed to sunlight, fish oils, milk products.	Rickets—defective bone formation; osteoporosis; weak/brittle bones.
Vitamin E	Maintenance of red blood cells. Acts as a potent antioxidant when combined with vitamin C.	Green leafy vegetables, seeds and nuts, egg yolk, avocado, whole grains.	Nerve and muscle damage.
Vitamin K	Synthesis of blood clotting factors; promotes bone health.	Dark-green leafy vegetables, cauliflower, cabbage.	Bruising and bleeding problems, slow clotting of blood.
Water-soluble vitamins			
Vitamin C	Acts as an antioxidant along with vitamin E. Helps in iron absorption. Plays a role in keeping immunity system strong.	Citrus fruits, tomatoes, cabbage, broccoli, potatoes, red/green/yellow bell peppers.	Scurvy—spontaneous haemorrhages, slow wound healing, swollen, bleeding gums.

Nutrient	Function	Sources	Deficiency symptoms
B-Complex vitamin group	Has a role in energy production, growth and health of red blood cells, required for healthy nerve and brain function, important for intestinal health and cardiovascular health. Also important in production of a few hormones, RNA and DNA, yielding energy from macronutrients. Supports strong bones and healthy skin.	Organ meat, fish, egg yolk, whole grains, germ, dark-green leafy vegetables, dairy products, nuts, legumes, avocado, cabbage, cauliflower.	Anaemia, low energy levels, skin disorders like dermatitis, pellagra, fissuring of skin, neuromotor disorders, cardiovascular disorders, hair loss.

6. Minerals

Minerals don't give energy to the body but perform many crucial roles in normal functioning of the body and to keep the body healthy. Body cannot produce minerals and that's why they should be included in the diet on a daily basis in required amounts. These are calcium, sodium, chloride, magnesium, phosphorus, iron, zinc, potassium, manganese, silicon, fluorine, molybdenum, cobalt, iodine, copper, boron, selenium, chromium. Among these there are a few minerals that the body requires in more amounts; therefore, they are known as macro minerals. The rest are micro minerals that the body requires in very less proportions.

To understand a few important minerals and their functions and deficiency symptoms, refer to the table below:

Nutrient	Functions	Sources	Deficiency symptoms
Calcium	Building bones and teeth, normal muscle function, heart muscle contraction, blood clotting.	Dairy products, leafy vegetables.	Weakening of bones, osteoporosis, tooth decay.
Phosphorus	Aids in bone and teeth formation, helps to maintain chemical balance of blood, plays a role in energy and strength production.	Peas, beans, milk products, broccoli, whole grains.	Brittle bones, 'peg leg', poor appetite.

Nutrient	Functions	Sources	Deficiency symptoms
Magnesium	Is a structural component of a bone. Is also an activator of enzyme reactions of carbohydrates' and fats' breakdown. Keeps heart muscles and nerves strong.	Available in almost all food items.	Nervous behaviour, twitching face and ear muscles.
Iron	Essential for oxygen transportation in red blood cells, used in cellular respiration, important for resistance to infection.	Liver, meat, peanuts, eggs, jaggery, dates, prunes, plums.	Anaemia, lack of stamina, poor immunity.
Sulphur	Component of the hormone, insulin and of several amino acids, builds hair, nails, skin.	Nuts, dried fruits, barley, oatmeal, eggs, beans.	Inability to digest roughage.

Nutrient	Functions	Sources	Deficiency symptoms
Potassium	Part of the system that controls acid–base and liquid balances, muscle contraction, transmission of nerve impulses	Bananas, citrus fruits, readily available in most foods.	Muscle cramping, dehydration, reduced weight gain, depraved appetite, muscular weakness.
Sodium	Regulates the fluid and acid–base balance of the body. Promotes healthy blood pressure. Regulates nervous system.	Table salt, milk, meat, fish, poultry.	Nausea, dizziness, poor concentration, muscle weakness.

FAQs

1. Do I have to eat less to lose weight?

To lose weight, you need to have nutrients as per your body requirements and your goals. You absolutely need not fast/ starve yourself to achieve weight loss.

2. Do I have to completely cut down on sugar during a weight loss programme?

All the carbohydrates (i.e., cereals, pulses, fruits) you eat get broken down into sugar (glucose) in your body. Your body doesn't need a simpler form of sugar (table sugar, honey) because enough sugar is available to your body throughout the day. Cutting down on simpler sugars gradually helps strengthen the immune system, muscle mass, skin health, etc.

3. Is it possible to get positive results despite some medical condition?

Yes. Most medical conditions (such as diabetes, hypertension, high cholesterol levels/abnormal lipid profile, etc.) are metabolic disorders caused due to poor lifestyle and poor dietary habits, thus leading to excessive weight gain. Gradual weight loss, in fact, helps in controlling these disorders.

4. Can a supplement or a fat burner help me lose weight?

If the diet is planned according to your goals and body's requirements, you will keep losing weight. There is no need to supplement your diet with a fat burner. Nevertheless, there are a few supplements (such as protein supplement, essential fatty acid supplement (Omega-3), multivitamins, etc.) that help in meeting our daily requirements of nutrients and have shown very good results in improving overall health.

5. Can a vegetarian build muscle mass?

Yes. Muscle-building is a gradual process that is achieved by consistent, progressive overload during workout and the support of a good, balanced diet. The diet can be rich in the protein sources that are easily available for the vegetarians. In case the daily requirement isn't completed even then, supplement support can also be given.

6. Is it possible to lose fat and gain muscles at the same time?

Yes. Along with a proper workout, even if you are following a fat-loss nutrition plan, there is always an improvement in strength that can be observed. Also, the more muscle gain is achieved, the easier it is for your body to cut fats, as muscles are metabolically active tissue in the body.

7. Is it possible to burn belly fat only through nutrition?

There is no spot reduction when it comes to nutrition and exercise. You start losing fats from all over your body. Thus, yes, you do lose belly fat with overall reduction in your body fat percentage through nutrition.

8. I am eating and exercising properly but not losing weight. What is the problem?

You need to look at the total amount of macronutrients that you require and the amount of macronutrients you are consuming. Most of the times, we don't eat according to the macros—we only look after the caloric count which can lead to no change in weight. Also, progressive overload during workout is equally important, which gives a challenge to your body every time you work out. If there isn't any challenge in the workout, it is very likely that no change in weight will be seen.

9. Why does weight loss seem to be tougher as you age?

Aging has an effect on your muscle mass. It leads to a lot of gradual muscle loss, thereby decreasing your metabolic rate. And this makes weight loss harder as you age. This can be simply avoided by having an active lifestyle with a good control over your diet.

10. Why is initial weight loss easier?

Glucose getting stored in your body leads to a lot of water retention. When you start losing weight, your glycogen stores are depleted for energy, thereby causing a decrease in the water mass stored in the body—which leads to weight loss. This is seen only in the initial phase of weight loss.

11. Does protein intake lead to kidney stone?

No. Proteins are required by your body on a daily basis as they perform various different functions in the body. Therefore, protein is an irreplaceable nutrient in the diet. Protein intake doesn't lead to kidney stones, but the patients suffering from kidney stones need to cut down protein in a particular amount from their diet.

12. Can I take protein when my uric acid is high?

Yes. High uric acid level is an outcome of high purine consumption. Purines are present in red meat, such as beef, pork, etc. As we don't consume red meat so often in India, the cause of high uric acid levels is often high-fructose, gluten and alcohol consumption—which has nothing to do with proteins. Therefore, you can have protein except red meat even if the uric acid levels are high.

13. I am trying to lose weight. Is skipping dinner or skipping a meal during the day a good way to lose?

Your body needs all the macronutrients and micronutrients on a daily basis throughout the day. You should avoid skipping any meals because it can also lead to excessive food consumption in the next meal, which will lead to fat gain. It will also lead to the metabolic rate being dropped, thereby converting the calories you've eaten to fats so that more energy is available in case of fasting.

14. What should be the time gap between two meals?

The ideal gap between two meals is 2–3 hours. This can vary according per individual depending on their schedule and suitability, though a gap of more than 4 hours is not recommended.

15. Is nutrition important to teenagers?

Yes. Adolescence is the period when the growth spurt is at its peak. That means the growth hormones are most active during this phase. Therefore, having an active lifestyle along with balanced nutrition will enhance the growth and development and will not lead to an obese adulthood.

16. What role does one's emotion play into nutrition?

Eating is closely tied to emotions. Eating to relieve tension or boredom can result in overeating. However, if you lose your appetite when you are upset or bored, you may miss getting essential nutrients. By understanding how eating relates to emotions, you can make more healthy food choices.

17. How many meals should I eat throughout the day?

This depends on a person's schedule and suitability and therefore varies from person to person. While the minimum number of meals you should be having is four, a person could have eight small meals as well. The target should be to complete all macronutrients and micronutrients requirements.

18. Is fasting a good way of losing weight?

For centuries, fasting has been part of the human social fabric. One of the most popular ways is intermittent fasting. Some of its studied benefits are balancing insulin levels, increasing human growth hormone levels and initiating cellular repair. So fasting the right way in a planned manner can help, but it is important to consult a dietician before taking up serious fasting.

Know your Body Type and Define Your 'Eat Well Plate'

Ectomorph - 25% Protein, 55% Carbs, 20% Fat
Mesomorph – 30% Protein 40% Carbs, 30% Fat
Endomorph – 35% Protein, 25% Carbs, 40% Fat

Sample Diet Plan

Food Calorie Note			
Time	**Food**	**Calories**	**Notes**
Around 7 a.m.	Pre-workout: • ½ scoop whey with water • 1 apple • black coffee/green tea Post workout: whey with water	288	
Around 10 a.m.	2 whole eggs 1 slice brown bread	360	Eggs omelette can be made using 1 tbsp ghee/ butter
Around 2 p.m.	• 100 gm cooked brown rice • 1 bowl spinach/green veggies • 100 gm rajma (cooked) • 1 bowl curd	350	
Around 5 p.m.	• A handful of dry fruits (almonds + walnuts) • ½ scoop whey	150	
Around 8 p.m.	• 1 multigrain roti (bajra + jowar + ragi) • 100 gm paneer/ chicken • Veggies	564	Paneer can be cooked into gravy using 1 tbsp ghee/butter

Total Calories = 1710

Are Carbohydrates Good or Bad?

Over the years there have been many experts and dietician suggesting cutting down on carbs drastically for weight management. One great concern about such a diet is the fact that many foods that have a high percentage of carbohydrates—such as fruit and whole grains—which are also the source of antioxidants. Antioxidants are the defence agents that help the body fight diseases.

Another concern with a very low carb diet is that such a diet tends to become low in fibre, which can cause problems with digestion.

And the biggest problem is that a diet severely low in carbs would be very difficult for anyone to follow for a lifetime. Also, humans are born with a preference for sweet foods.

However, if you have been having mostly carbohydrates, it will eventually lead to increase in fat due to insulin resistance.

How Insulin Turns On Your Fat Switch

Carbohydrates are your body's main source of energy. They include all sugars and honey, all fruits, and all starchy foods, such as bread, cereals, pasta, grains, rice, potatoes and corn. All carbohydrates are broken down during digestion into sugars. Every one of your body's cell needs glucose to function. Insulin is the regulator of your blood glucose levels. Insulin is a hormone, just like oestrogen and testosterone, thyroid and cortisol. After you eat carbohydrates, your blood glucose levels rise and the pancreas normally respond by releasing insulin. If you have more in your body than your cells need, the insulin takes the extra blood glucose and transports it into fat storage. So insulin's job is to regulate blood glucose and store excess glucose as fat. When insulin rises and spikes to regulate blood sugar levels, then more fat is also being stored. In seeking the real fat loss solution, the question is: 'If higher insulin level makes you fat, then does lower insulin level make you thin?' The answer is: Yes. Keeping insulin levels from spiking is the key to your weight loss solution and is the basis of a balanced eating method.

Balanced Protein and Carbohydrates

Studies have shown that protein-rich foods do not cause insulin to spike. Eating fat and carbohydrates also delays rise in insulin, but it will not help in weight loss. This is because fat contains more than twice as many calories as protein and carbohydrate. You must balance every one serving of carbohydrate food with one serving of high-protein food.

Concern about High-Protein, High-Fat and Low-Carb Diet

It is important to be aware that a high-protein and high-fat diet carries the risk of a medical condition called Ketoacidosis. Ketogenesis, or the production of ketones, occurs when carbohydrate intake drops to less than 50 g per day. A ketogenic diet or a keto diet is the new fad diet to lose fat. However, these by-products of fat metabolism can be very damaging to the body and can even result in ketoacidosis. In this state, the body's acid–base balance is distributed by the acid level of these ketone bodies. Also high-fat foods do not provide enough satiety signals.

Myths

1. High-protein diets lead to kidney dysfunction

Although protein-restricted diets are helpful for people who already have kidney disease, eating high proteins does not cause kidney problems. Indeed, the fat-soluble vitamins and fatty acids found in animal foods are essential for properly functioning kidneys.

2. Fats are bad for health

Good fats are required by the body on a day-to-day basis for different functions. Bad fats like trans fats and hydrogenated fats should not be consumed as they increase risk to healthy well-being.

3. Cardio is better than weight training

Weight training burns calories even after workout, during the recovery phase, and tones up the muscles, thereby the body also improves strength.

4. Whey protein is not good for health

One of the most prominent myths is that whey protein contains steroids. However, the fact is that whey protein is cow's milk, is 100 per cent vegetarian and helps in faster recovery and builds muscle mass due to its bioavailability of being absorbed in the body faster and rebuilding strength and mass.

5. Crash dieting gives good results

Many people are under the impression that the lower you drop your calories, the better result you'll see. While this may be true in the short term, crash dieting can be dangerous in the long run. Fat loss efforts end up gaining the weight back, plus more—ultimately increasing your weight. Hence, there is no need to resort an extreme approach to improve your body composition.

Glossary of Fitness Terms

Activities of Daily Living (ADLs): Physical tasks of everyday living, such as bathing, and walking up the stairs. ADLs are usually factored in to a person's basal metabolic rate, so tracking calories burned for these types of movement is not recommended when trying to lose weight.

Aerobic exercise: Any rhythmic activity that increases the body's need for oxygen by using large muscle groups continuously for at least 10 minutes. The term aerobic means 'with oxygen'.

Agonist muscle: A muscle that is very effective in causing a certain joint movement. Also called the prime mover. On a biceps curl, the biceps is the agonist muscle that flexes the elbow joint.

Amenorrhea: The absence of menstruation, commonly found in women with a very low body fat percentage and/or in those who exercise excessively.

Anaerobic exercise: Short-lasting, high-intensity activity, where the demand for oxygen from the exercise exceeds the oxygen supply.

Antagonist muscle: A muscle that causes movement at a joint in a direction opposite to that of the joint's agonist (prime mover).

Beta-blockers: Type of medication that reduces heart rate. Exercisers who take beta-blockers will have a lower heart rate at rest and during exercise.

Body composition: Amount of fat versus lean muscle tissue in the human body.

Body mass index (BMI): Measure of the relationship between height and weight; calculated by dividing weight in kilograms by height in centimetres squared.

Caffeine: A stimulant found in coffee, tea, chocolate, and some soft drinks, which increases heart contractions, oxygen consumption, metabolism and urinary output.

Calisthenics: Exercising using one's own body weight, which helps develop muscular tone.

Cardiorespiratory fitness: Measure of the heart's ability to pump oxygen-rich blood to the muscles. Also called cardiovascular or aerobic fitness.

Cardiovascular system: A complex system consisting of the heart and blood vessels; transports nutrients, oxygen and enzymes throughout the body and regulates temperature, water levels of cells and acidity levels of body components.

Circuit training: Takes the participant through a series of exercise stations (which could also include strength training), with relatively brief rest intervals between each station. The purpose is to keep the heart rate elevated near the aerobic level without dropping. The number of stations may range from 4 to 10.

Concentric muscle action: Force produced while the muscle is shortening in length.

Continuous training: This is the most common type of sustained aerobic exercise for fitness improvement, slowly adding more time to the workout to increase endurance.

Cool down: Lowering of body temperature following vigorous exercise. The practice of cooling down after exercise involves slowing down your level of activity gradually.

Core: A muscle group comprised of the abdominals, lower back, obliques and hips.

Cross-training: An individualized combination of all aerobic-training methods, characterized by a variety of intensities and modes.

Detraining principle: This principle says that once consistent exercise stops, you will eventually lose the strength that you built up. Without overload or maintenance, muscles will weaken in two weeks or less.

Diastolic blood pressure: The pressure exerted by the blood on the vessel walls during the resting portion of the cardiac cycle, measured in millimetres of mercury. The diastolic number is the bottom of the fraction. 120/80 is an average value for normal blood pressure (80 is the diastolic number). Mild high blood pressure is considered to be between 140/90 and 160/95. High blood pressure is defined by a value greater than 160/95.

Delayed onset muscle soreness (DOMS): Muscle soreness or discomfort that appears 12–48 hours after exercise. It is most likely due to microscopic tears in the muscle tissue, and it usually requires a couple of days for the repair and rebuilding process to be completed. The muscle tissue grows back stronger, leading to increased muscle mass and strength.

Eccentric contraction: A lengthening of the muscle during its contraction; controls speed of movement caused by another force.

Ectomorph: A body shape characterized by a narrow chest, narrow shoulders and long, thin muscles.

Endomorph: A body shape characterized by a round face, short neck , wide hips, and heavy fat storage.

Endorphins: Opiate-like hormones that are manufactured in the body and which contribute to natural feelings of well-being.

Excess post-exercise oxygen consumption (EPOC): This explains why your breathing rate remains heavy for a few minutes after finishing a workout. Your body needs more oxygen after a workout in order to restore the oxygen stores in the blood and tissues, and to meet the oxygen requirements of the heart rate, which is still elevated.

Epinephrine: Also called adrenaline, a hormone that stimulates body systems in response to stress.

Exercise metabolic rate (EMR): The energy expenditure that occurs during exercise.

Fast twitch muscle fibres: Fibres that are better suited to high-force, short-duration activities because they contain more stores for anaerobic energy utilization.

Fixed resistance: Strength-training exercises that provide a constant amount of resistance throughout the full range of motion. Examples include free weights and resistance bands.

Flexibility: The measure of the range of motion, or the amount of movement possible, at a particular joint.

Heart rate reserve (HRR): The difference between resting and maximal heart rate.

Heat cramps: Muscle cramps that occur during or following exercise in warm or hot weather.

Heat exhaustion: A heat stress illness caused by significant dehydration resulting from exercise in warm or hot conditions; frequent precursor to heat stroke.

Heat stroke: A deadly heat stress illness resulting from dehydration and overexertion in warm or hot conditions; can cause body core temperature to rise from normal to 100° or 105° Fahrenheit in just a few minutes.

High-density lipoprotein (HDL): Retrieves cholesterol from the body's cells and returns it to the liver to be metabolized. Also referred to as 'good' cholesterol.

High impact: Activities that place more stress on the bones and joints, where your limbs are actually making contact with the ground or other surface with force. Examples include walking, running, step aerobics, and sports that involve impact, like basketball or tennis.

Hyperplasia: An increase in the number of cells in a tissue, usually in reference to fat or muscle cells.

Hypertrophy: An increase in cell size (girth), usually in reference to fat or muscle cells.

Hypothermia: A life-threatening condition in which heat is lost from the body faster than it is produced.

Incremental exercise test (Graded exercise test): An exercise test involving a progressive increase in work rate over time. Often these tests are used to determine the subject's maximum oxygen consumption or lactic threshold.

Interval training: Repeated intervals of exercise interspersed with intervals of relatively light exercise. This type of training provides a means of performing large amounts of high-intensity exercise in a short period of time.

Isokinetic exercise: Exercise in which the rate of movement is constantly maintained through a specific range of motion even though maximal force is exerted.

Isometric exercise: Any activity in which the muscles exert force but do not visibly change in length. For example, pushing against a wall or carrying a bag of groceries.

Isotonic exercise: Any activity in which the muscles exert force and change in length as they lift and lower resistance. For example, bicep curls or leg extensions.

Ketosis: A condition in which the body adapts to prolonged fasting or carbohydrate deprivation by converting body fat to ketones—which can be used as fuel for some brain activity. The real danger in ketosis is that ketones are acidic, and high levels of ketones make the blood abnormally acidic.

Lactic acid: Once thought of as a waste substance that builds up in the muscles when they are not getting enough oxygen, leading to muscle fatigue and soreness. Now, experts believe that lactic acid is beneficial to the body, acting as a 'fuel' to help people continue high-intensity (anaerobic) exercise even when oxygen consumption is low.

Lactic threshold: The point at which the level of lactic acid in the blood suddenly increases (during exercise). This is a good indication of the highest sustainable work rate. Also known as anaerobic threshold.

Lean mass: Total weight of your muscle, bone and all other body organs (everything in the body excluding fat).

Low-density lipoprotein (LDL): Transports cholesterol and triglycerides from the liver to be used in various cellular processes. Also referred to as 'bad' cholesterol.

Low impact: Activities that place less stress on the bones and joints. These are better for people with joint pain, and overweight individuals whose weight can hurt their joints. Examples include swimming, elliptical, cycling, and other activities where your feet (or other body parts) aren't touching the ground with force or where you are somehow supported.

Max VO 2 (V02 Max): The highest amount of oxygen one can consume during exercise. The higher this number, the more cardiovascularly fit you are and thus capable of increased levels of intensity.

Mesomorph: A body shape characterized by a large chest, long torso, solid muscle structure and significant strength.

Moderate intensity: Activities that range from 40 per cent to 60 per cent of maximum heart rate. These activities cause a slightly increased rate of breathing, and feel light to somewhat difficult. Individuals doing activity at this intensity can easily carry on a conversation.

Muscle fibres: Individual muscle cells that are the functional components of muscles.

Muscular endurance: The ability of the muscle to perform repetitive contractions over a prolonged period of time.

Muscular strength: The ability of the muscle to generate the maximum amount of force.

Obesity: A weight disorder generally defined as an accumulation of fat beyond that considered normal for a person based on age, sex and body type.

One-Rep Max (1 RM): The amount of weight/resistance that can be lifted or moved once, but not twice—a common measure of strength.

Opposing muscles: Muscles that work in opposition to the ones you are training. For example, the bicep is the opposing muscle to the triceps; the hamstring is the opposing muscle to the quadriceps.

Osteoporosis: A disease characterized by low bone mass and deterioration of bone tissue, which increases risk of fracture.

Overload principle: This principle says that in order to train muscles, they must work harder than they are accustomed to. This 'overload' will result in increased strength as the body adapts to the stress placed upon it.

Overuse injuries: Injuries that result from the cumulative effects of repetitive (day-after-day) stresses placed on tendons, muscles and joints.

Per cent grade: Measure of the elevation of a treadmill.

Physical fitness: The ability to perform regular to vigorous physical activity without great fatigue.

Pilates: Exercise programmes that combine dynamic stretching with movement against resistance.

Plateau: Point in an exercise programme where no additional progress is being made (gains in strength, weight loss, increased endurance, etc.). One way to break through a plateau is to change the kind of activity you are doing or something about your current activity: adding hills, increasing speed, increasing distance, etc.

PNF stretching: Proprioceptive neuromuscular facilitation (PNF) stretching is a static stretch of a muscle immediately after maximally contracting it.

Primary prevention: Actions designed to stop problems before they start.

Pronation: To turn or rotate (the foot) so that the inner edge of the sole bears the body's weight.

Plyometric training: Exercises that enable a muscle to reach maximal force production in as short a time as possible. For example, jumping from a 3-foot stool to the ground and immediately springing back up to another stool.

Rate of perceived exertion (RPE): Scale of 1–10 that rates how you are feeling (both physically and mentally) as it relates to exercise fatigue.

Repetition: The number of times an exercise is repeated within a single exercise 'set'.

Resistance training: See 'strength training'.

Resting heart rate: Rate at which your heart beats at rest (while sitting or being inactive). Low resting heart rates are a good measure of health and fitness.

Resting metabolic rate (RMR): Number of calories expended to maintain the body during resting conditions. Also referred to as basal metabolic rate.

Set: A basic unit of a workout containing the number of times (repetitions) a specific exercise is done (e.g., 3 sets of 5 repetitions with 100 pounds).

Shin splint: Generic term used to describe pain in the lower leg, either on the medial (inside) or lateral side (outside) of the shin bone.

Sit and reach test: A common fitness test that determines flexibility (of the hamstrings and lower back).

Skinfold calliper test: A method of determining body fat whereby folds of skin and fat at various points on the body are grasped between thumb and forefinger and measured with callipers.

Skin fold measurements: This method of measuring body composition assumes that substantial fat is proportional to overall body fat, and thus by measuring several sites, total body fat may be calculated.

Slow twitch muscle fibres: Fibres that are better suited to low-force, long-duration activities because they possess more endurance enzymes.

Specificity of training principle: This principle says that only the muscle or muscle group you exercise will respond to the demands placed upon it. By regularly doing curls, for example, the muscles involved (biceps) will become larger and stronger, but curls will have no effect on the muscles that are not being trained. Therefore, in strength training, it is important to strengthen all of the major muscles.

Static stretching: A low-force, high-duration stretch where the muscle is held at the greatest possible length for up to 30 seconds.

Strength training (resistance training): The process of exercising with progressively heavier resistance for the purpose of strengthening the musculoskeletal system.

Systolic blood pressure: The pressure exerted on the vessel walls during ventricular contraction, measured in millimetres of mercury. The systolic number is the top of the fraction. 120/80 is an average value for normal blood pressure (120 is the systolic number). Mild high blood pressure is considered to be between 140/90 and 160/95. High blood pressure is defined by a value greater than 160/95.

Tapering: The process athletes use to reduce their training load for several days prior to competition.

Target heart rate (THR): The recommended range is 60–85 per cent of your maximum heart rate. It represents a pace that ensures you are training aerobically and can reasonably be maintained.

Testosterone: The steroid hormone produced in the testes; involved in growth and development of muscle mass. Since men have more testosterone than women, they are able to gain muscle mass more easily.

Thyroid: Endocrine gland located in the neck that secretes T3 and T4 (hormones), which increase metabolic rate.

Type-I muscle fibres: Fibres that contain large quantities of oxidative enzymes and are highly fatigue-resistant (more prevalent in endurance athletes).

Type-II A muscle fibres: Fibres that contain biochemical and fatigue characteristics that are between Type-II B and Type-I fibres (the best of both worlds).

Type-II B muscle fibres: Fibres that have a relatively small number of mitochondria, a limited capacity for aerobic metabolism, and are less resistant to fatigue than slow fibres (more prevalent in sprinters and power lifters).

Variable resistance: Strength-training exercises that change the amount of resistance throughout the full range of motion.

Vigorous intensity: Activities above 60 per cent of max heart rate. These activities cause an increased rate of breathing and sweating, and feel somewhat difficult to quite tough.

Waist to hip ratio: A calculation of the proportion of fat stored on your body around your waist and hips. Formula: waist measurement divided by hip measurement. Women should have a ratio of 0.8 or less; men should have a ratio of .95 or less.

Warm up: To prepare for an athletic event (whether a game or a workout session) by exercising, stretching, or practising for a short time beforehand.

Yoga: A genre of Indian exercises called asanas, geared towards self-discipline and the realization of harmony of body and mind; includes forms of exercise that promote balance, coordination, flexibility and meditation.